Is there ANYONE better than HENRIETTA?

Martine Murray

ALLEN&UNWIN
SYDNEY · MELBOURNE · AUCKLAND · LONDON

ACKNOWLEDGEMENTS

I would like to acknowledge the invaluable work of Verity Prideaux in the making of Henrietta. Without you and your glorious patterns and textures, Henrietta would have had a very drab take-off. Thanks also to Rosalind Price, Sue Flockhart and the original and best squidger, Sally Rippin.

This bind-up edition of *Henrietta: There's No One Better*, *Henrietta the Great Go-Getter*, *Henrietta Gets a Letter* and *Henrietta and the Perfect Night* first published by Allen & Unwin in 2022

Copyright © *Henrietta: There's No One Better,* Martine Murray 2004
Copyright © *Henrietta the Great Go-Getter*, Martine Murray 2006
Copyright © *Henrietta Gets a Letter*, Martine Murray 2008
Copyright © *Henrietta and the Perfect Night*, Martine Murray 2017

All rights reserved. No part of this book may be reproduced or transmitted in any form or by any means, electronic or mechanical, including photocopying, recording or by any information storage and retrieval system, without prior permission in writing from the publisher. The Australian *Copyright Act 1968* (the Act) allows a maximum of one chapter or ten per cent of this book, whichever is the greater, to be photocopied by any educational institution for its educational purposes provided that the educational institution (or body that administers it) has given a remuneration notice to the Copyright Agency (Australia) under the Act.

Allen & Unwin
83 Alexander Street
Crows Nest NSW 2065
Australia
Phone: (61 2) 8425 0100
Email: info@allenandunwin.com
Web: www.allenandunwin.com

 A catalogue record for this book is available from the National Library of Australia

ISBN 978 1 76106 718 1

For teaching resources, explore www.allenandunwin.com/resources/for-teachers

Illustration technique: pencil and ink drawing, with gouache colour added electronically

Cover design by Sandra Nobes
Cover illustrations by Martine Murray: Henrietta on spine © 2006,
newly coloured 2022; rest of cover images © 2008
Text design by Martine Murray and Verity Prideaux (books 1–3) and Sandra Nobes (book 4)
Page i titlepage illustration © Martine Murray 2008;
page 380 puppy illustration © Martine Murray 2017
Set in 13 pt Sabon by Verity Prideaux (books 1–3) and 15 pt Jenson Classico
by Sandra Nobes (book 4)

This book was printed in January 2022 by C&C Offset Printing Co., Ltd, China

1 3 5 7 9 10 8 6 4 2

www.martinemurray.com

Contents

Henrietta: There's No One Better   1

Henrietta the Great Go-Getter   97

Henrietta Gets a Letter   193

Henrietta and the Perfect Night   289

AWARDS

Henrietta: There's No One Better

- Shortlisted, Patricia Wrightson Prize,
NSW Premier's Literary Awards, 2005

- Shortlisted, Best Book for Language Development,
Speech Pathology Australia Book of the Year Awards, 2005

- Shortlisted, Best Designed Children's Picture Book,
53rd APA Book Design Awards, 2005

Henrietta and the Perfect Night

- Honour Book, Younger Readers category,
CBCA Book of the Year Awards, 2018

PRAISE

'Brimming with charm and originality.' *The Sunday Age*

'Filled with the joy of living.' *Good Reading*

'For the small, the joyous and those ready for adventure.' *The Bulletin*

'Off-the-wall.' *Women's Weekly*

'Highly recommended.' *Magpies*

'Captivating.' *New Zealand Herald*

'Heaps of fun.' *dMag*

'A great read.' Charlotte (8) in *The Sunday Tasmanian*

'A book to help young imaginations soar.' *Junior*

'Irresistible.' *Australian Education Union News*

HENRIETTA

There's No One Better

*Henrietta P. Hoppenbeek would like this book
to be dedicated to the Wonderful Witches of Westgarth,
Nessie Noo, Cal E. Wag and Emsie T.*

*And also to Squeezy and Clare Bear,
and to Clive and Pete and Hobbit, and Nigelo
and Rico and Broni and Soni and Beast and the
faraway but ever near Jennie Higgie.*

*But that seems like a lot of people, so instead
this book is dedicated to the friends you have
lived with and the family they are to you.*

Henrietta P. Hoppenbeek *the first*

Allow me to introduce myself properly. I am Henrietta P. Hoppenbeek the First, future Queen of the Wide Wide Long Cool Coast of the Lost Socks, and the only person in the even Wider World to have visited the Island of the Rietta.

Don't forget that, because when I do become Queen, you may just want to ask me for a sunny part of the kingdom to lie about in with your dog. You never know.

Anyone who knows me well can call me Henri. But only if you know me really well, and not if you pull my hair like Bartley Baker does.

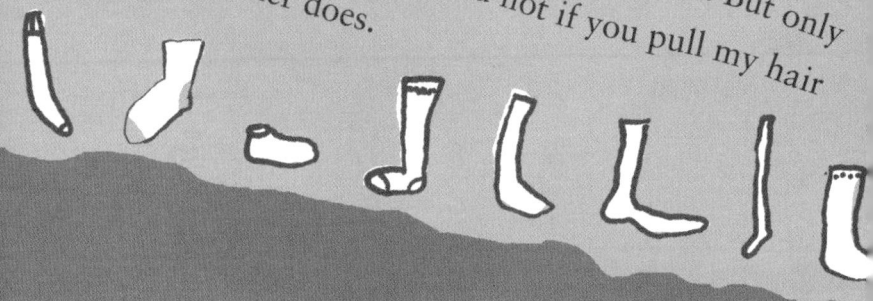

I'm a good wiggler, and sometimes

I'm *exhillperating* and sometimes I'm *expasperating*

 I have a brother called Albert,
but he's only the size of a sock.

Not really.
He's probably about the same size
as a sewing machine,
only he can't sew.

a not-at-all,
not-one-bit
best friend
called Bartley
Baker

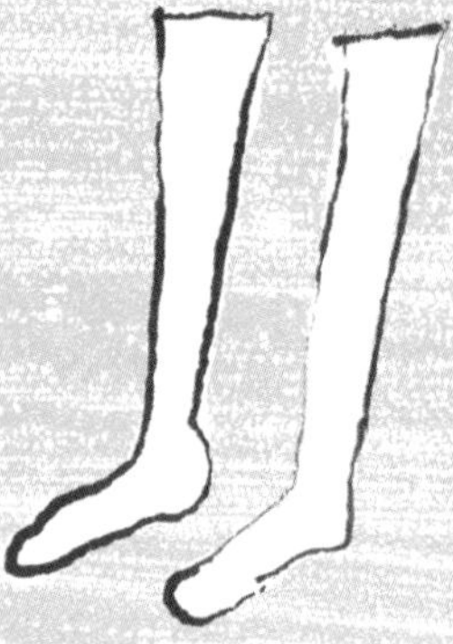

I have a mad brown dog called Madge,

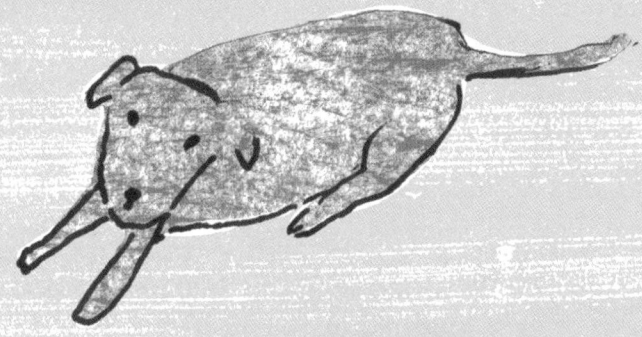

two white mice called Flora and Dora,

a best friend called Olive Higgie,
hair like spaghetti,
a diamond crown,
a woolly mammoth,
long green socks
and a big bad habit of making things up.

(I don't really have a woolly mammoth.)

It's only Madge wearing a woolly mammoth coat

Way too many Alberts

Luckily, there's only one Albert in our family.
If there were more than one,
that would be way too many Alberts.
Can you imagine a whole house full of Alberts?

Alberts on the bookshelf,

Alberts in the washing machine,

Alberts in the shoe cupboard,

Alberts in the sink,

Alberts
in the lounge room,
slouching on the couch,

Alberts in the veggie patch,
crouching on the cabbage,

Alberts on the tellie and Alberts on the phone,

Alberts under my feet and Alberts on my nerves.

Oh boy, in a house full of Alberts there'd be a whole lot of howling and sleeping and burping and not many chocolate ripple cakes getting cooked and nothing being invented.

That's why it's lucky I'm here.
To make sure things keep happening.
Like when Mum is trying to put Albert to sleep,
I play the drums in the kitchen.
When I bang the end of the wooden spoon
on the wok it sounds like cracking thunder
and it makes my mum come running
with her face all screwed up, making

shhhhh   shhhhh

noises, which go quite well with the drums.

She says, Henrietta, you're exasperating!

It's because I'm better at drumming than she is.
Mum only knows how to make *shhhh* noises.
Dad sometimes plays guitar,
but Mum says he only knows three songs
and she's sick of them.

Here's what I can do

I can ride the chair to Africa.
Or I can become a very
astounding statue.
I can become a duelling rhinoceros,
a surf champion,
a prehistoric tortoise,
an acrobat, a bushranger
or a high-and-mighty lady
singing hallelujah,
praise the land of agreeable chairs.
I can keep a secret,
I can make my dad's undies
into an absolutely superb hat,
I can play chair guitar and
then I can slam all the doors
in the whole house
before you can say,
'Oh my Lord, Henrietta,
do you have to make such a racket?'
I can lean back and let it all come easy.

I reckon I could even convince
a woolly mammoth to shampoo his hair.
Don't worry, when Albert is old enough
I'll teach him everything I know,
except how to reach the biscuit tin.

I can't really keep a secret.

Here's what I want to be

Not a king,
because kings
can't fart.
And not a soldier,
because they have
to take orders
and walk all stiff.

And not a mother, because they have to clean up.

yuk

And not a dad, because they have to clean up too.

And especially not a dentist,
because if you were a dentist
no one would want
to come and see you.
Not unless they had a toothache.
What kind of guest is that?
Not a fun one, I can tell you.

Maybe I would like to be a cloud,
but I can't be sure.
I know I would like to be superb,
like Uncle George's new car,

and occasionally a genius,

but not so much
that the world
would depend on me
to invent something
in a crisis.

What I really want to be is an explorer.

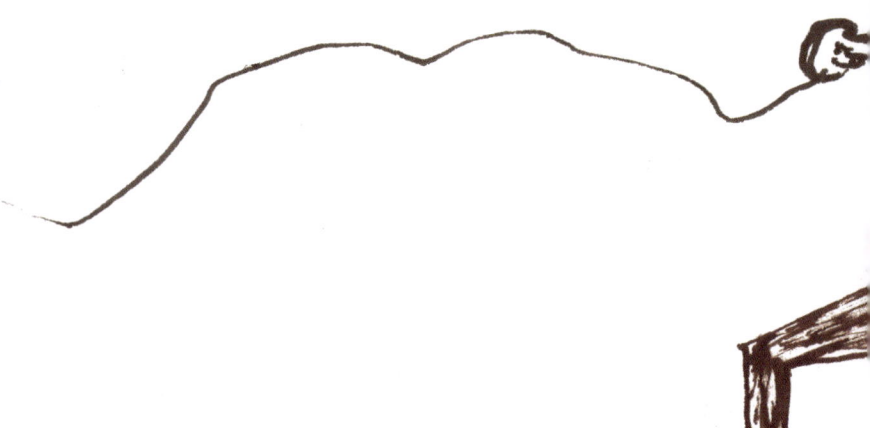

Explorification

I practise every day.
What I like doing best is walking BIG steps without looking.

I always leave a trail behind me.

Just in case.

But it's best before dinner time,
when I get in the bath
and sail the bathtub
to undiscovered lands
without snakes.

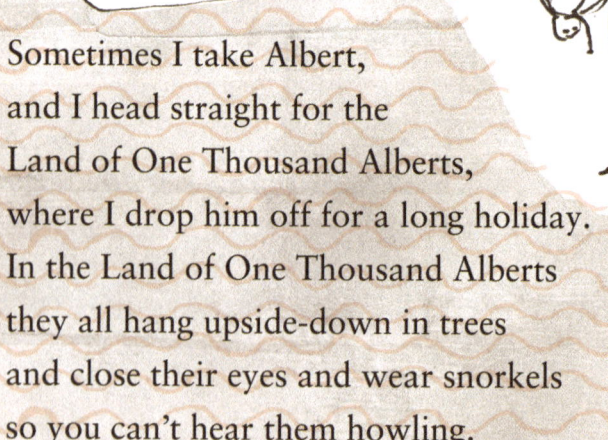

Sometimes I take Albert,
and I head straight for the
Land of One Thousand Alberts,
where I drop him off for a long holiday.
In the Land of One Thousand Alberts
they all hang upside-down in trees
and close their eyes and wear snorkels
so you can't hear them howling.

You can only hear very superb songs sung
by a host of invisible lady singers from Budapest.
Then I look out for the
Wide Wide Long Cool Coast of the Lost Socks.

It's lucky Mum doesn't come with me,
because she would definitely bring
all the lost socks home
and put them back into pairs.
But me, I just wave and wiggle
at the naughty escaper socks
and leave them to be individuals
under the palm trees.

On my way,
I sail past a Pelican
standing on a rock.
The Pelican is wearing a red raincoat
and he flaps his wings every now and then,
just to make sure you don't mistake him
for a very small lighthouse
or a mushroom.
He can't open his beak, though,
because he has something
inside.

I know what it is.

A **naughty** word.
Like what Dad says
when Madge takes his shoe
and gives it a good chew
in the back garden
and leaves it there,
lost and wet and squashed
and covered in dog slobber.

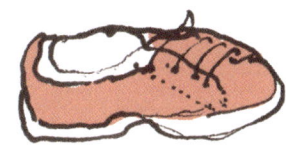

Meet the Rietta

By far the best land I go to
is the Island of the Rietta.
I bet you've never even heard of a Rietta.
In fact, I might be the only single person
who has ever seen one.
That's because I have a special relationship
with the Rietta.
See, I'm Henrietta,
that's half a Hen and half a Rietta.

Everyone knows what hens are,
because they squawk a lot and carry on,
but no one has ever seen a Rietta.
No one except me, of course.

A Rietta isn't quite an animal and it isn't
quite a person and it isn't quite a piece of furniture
or an antique car, either,
in case you were thinking it might be.
A grown-up Rietta has big blotchy spots,
but a baby one has small dotty dots.
A Rietta only eats chocolate ripple biscuits.
It never eats brussel sprouts, never.
And it likes to wear a cake tin on its head,
in case a chocolate ripple cake
should fall from the sky.
A Rietta gets sad if you leave it alone
or say mean things to it. On the other hand,
if you play with a Rietta for a while
its naughty nature rubs off on you
and you end up doing naughty things,
like jumping on the bed and making a hullabaloo.
A Rietta tends to be confused and sometimes lonely,
but it always makes the best of things.
So, if you see one,
be sure to say something encouraging like…

Oh, what spectacular

spots you have!

And also be sure to play with it,
because all Riettas like to play.

When I park my bath,
the Rietta trots up and looks inside,
because Riettas always hope for presents.
They can't help it. I always bring a pillow,
and the Rietta eats a hole in the pillow and throws
all the feathers in the air and starts to laugh.
It doesn't squawk, it makes oink noises like a pig.
Then it gets tired and lies down
and expects me to tickle its tummy with a feather,
just like Mum sometimes does to me
when I'm going to sleep.
I don't drum for the sleeping Rietta,
I sing Rock My Soul, and the Rietta smiles
and hoots every now and then in appreciation.
Then I row my bath back to the bathroom where
Mum is always waiting with a big furry towel.
Don't worry, on the way I go to the
Land of One Thousand upside-down Alberts
and pick up our Albert,
because Mum would be mad if I left him
hanging in the tree.

Tickling Albert

I am standing by the heater in the nuddy.
I'm getting dry before I pop on my pyjamas,
of course.
And all of a sudden
I hear that Pelican on the rock,
opening his beak
and letting out
that word.

It isn't what my dad says,
after all, it's what I say
when I stand too close
to the heater
with my bare bottom…

sheezama

geeza

At bedtime
I give Albert a little friendly tickle,
to see if he hoots like the Rietta.
But he doesn't hoot, he just gurgles.

One day I might even take him with me,
when he's old enough.
We might just discover another land together.
Possibly the Land of the Grumpy Potatoes,
where I will lie down and some stray feathers
from the Island of the Rietta will fall from the sky
and land very softly on my eyelids,
so softly I can hardly even feel them...

List of Undiscovered Lands

Land of squashy and spiky things
Land of the fat wombat called Graham
Land made of bird poo
Land where only very rude people live
Land ruled by a LARGE old sunburnt nose
Land where legs get lazy
Land that feels like a bean bag
Land where nothing adds up
Land of larger-than-you-can-ever-imagine
Land of the grumpy potatoes and the half-hearted army of brussel sprouts

My dad's like my dog

Dad's alarm wakes me up. It doesn't wake Dad up,
even though it beeps right next to his ear.
I think his ear is getting tired of hearing.
Mum elbows him in his side,
but he just snorts because he's used to that.

So I let Madge in, and we jump on the bed
and Madge licks Dad on the face,
and that usually wakes him up.
Madge is brown all over except for her tongue,
which is pink. My dad isn't brown all over,
and his name isn't Madge,
but in some particular ways he's just like Madge.
(Don't tell him I said that.)

Dad

Madge

For one thing, both Madge and Dad have an office.
Dad's office is in the city,
Madge's office is in the backyard.

Dad's office is a room with a desk and a computer and some empty old coffee cups.

Madge's office is that squashed patch of grass under the tree which is covered in rotten stinky bones and old cans and bits of hose.

Mainly what Madge does in her office is chew stuff, especially if it looks threatening,
like a hose.

Mainly what Dad does in his office is read stuff, especially if it's about golf.

Once, it was Dad's birthday,
but no one remembered.

Not even Dad.

He went to his office,
because somebody's got to earn a crust,
and Mum went into the garage
to make bowls out of clay, because she's an artist,
and Alfred had a nap, because he's a baby,
and I made a cushion castle,
because I'm an inventor.

But then Madge got bored,
because she's a crazy brown dog
who needs a lot of patting,
so she went to work in her office,
and I definitely had to help her,
because someone has to make sure
things around here get done
properly.

First, she got a cushion off the couch
and then she dragged it out to her office,
where she pretended it was a wild animal.
She got it in her mouth
and she shook it and leapt around
as if the cushion was attacking her.
It was just like what Dad does with a cushion
when he's watching the footy on tellie,
especially when the Tigers are losing.

When Madge had triumphed over the cushion,
she chewed it up
and left white bits of stuffing
all over her office,
and it looked like it had been snowing.

Then Madge and I both caught a whiff of something in the air...

Mum was cooking, and thank my lucky

and doubly thank my lucky stars

No, it was a much MUCH

It was the best thing possible, a thing that make

chocolate

I ran inside. First I said, ripper

can I lick the bowl? and then, lastly

It was a birthday

tars above, it wasn't kidney bean stew

bove, it wasn't even brussel sprouts.

ore thrilling thing.

ettas very, very excited. You guessed it:

ipple cake

hen I said, what's going on?

aid, please, which always ups your chances.

ake for Dad.

Then Mum saw the remains of the cushion
in Madge's office, and I was glad it was Madge
who did it and not me because Mum wasn't happy,
I can tell you.
Madge was heading for a whopping big smack,
but luckily for Madge there's one whiff in the air
that's even better than chocolate,
and that's rubbish.

Madge always runs away
on rubbish day.
She can't help herself.
She jumps the fence
and scurries off
to roam the streets
and plunder bins
and roll in the stinkiest stuff
she can find.

We all waited for Madge and Dad
to come home.

Albert had banana and gurgled on the floor

Mum sat cross-legged and said, Omm
It calms her down.
I watched tellie. It calms me down.

We waited and we waited…
Mum said she was getting a headache.
I said I was getting a bellyache.
(That's the pain you get when you can smell chocolate cake but you're not supposed to eat it.)

Where was Dad?

And more importantly,
was that chocolate cake feeling lonely and unloved
sitting all alone in the kitchen
while Mum had her eyes closed?

Dad got home first.
He was singing Happy Birthday to himself.
Mum wouldn't kiss him because he smelt like a pub.
Then Madge came home.
Mum told Madge to go outside because she stank
of rubbish and she'd destroyed a cushion.
I said, 'Happy Birthday, Dad,'
and he gave me a kiss, even though he was smelly.
Then Mum went to get the cake.
It had disappeared.
Right off the kitchen table.

poof

Just like that. Gone!
Where do you think it had gone? I'll tell you.
First it went into Madge's office.
And then it went into Madge's stomach.
That's the other thing Dad and Madge
have in common: they both can't resist chocolate.
Only Madge doesn't get a tummy bulging
over her pants, like Dad does.
But then Madge doesn't wear pants.

When they're in trouble,
Dad and Madge sit on the verandah.
But when they're out of trouble
there's one place they both like to be.

On the couch.

Lucky it's a big couch.

How to become an animal

Okay, there are two rules:

1. Best time to become an animal is on weekends

2. But don't do it if your dad has a headache or if Albert is sleeping

While it's easier to become an animal
than it is to become an astronaut,
let me tell you, it's not as simple as hiding
a green pea in your nostril…

First of all, you definitely must get dirty.

If you want
to become an animal
you can't worry
about getting
mud on your knees,

or leaves that
stickers to your knickers,

or wet on your bum,

or knots in your hair.

That's all part of the job.

Second of all, for no apparent reason you can howl.
Especially if the world seems contradictory…
if it's raining just when you want to go outside.
I open my heart and howl,
and Albert sometimes joins in, and Mum says,

Oh my Lord, must you?

So I dash upstairs and get glamorous instead.
And, when I'm supposed to eat
brussel sprouts or kidney bean stew,
I give it a reluctant sniff and turn up my nose.
And when I eat ice-cream,
I'm a much MUCH nicer animal.
And, sometimes, just sometimes, after lunch,
just because Albert has to snooze,
I come across a small moment of idleness.

But afterwards, look out!

The sun is shining again
and I'm getting all wriggly and jumpy.

What I imagine is, if I run fast enough up the

I might just take off

road and down the green hill,

And then again, I might not.

It doesn't matter.
If the sky is blue enough,
I absolutely
must sing about it
anyway.

Here's what I sing:
'Well, I'm Henrietta
and I've got long green socks with toes
and a little brother called Albert
who only knows one word

fish'

And when I'm very pleased with myself,

I dance like a wild thing.

And if I can't think
of what else to do,
I simply
astonish myself.
I turn the world up
the other way.

At the end of the day, when my tummy is rumbling,
I go inside and purr at Mum,
who is making spaghetti for dinner.
She says, Henrietta,
no sticking peas up your nostrils and
no writing rude words with the spaghetti

But I'm too hungry
to think about
hiding peas
or writing

sheezamageeza

Oh Lordy Lordy,
I'm as hungry
as a bungry,
and don't ask me
what a bungry is
because that's
another story.

Flora and Dora

In my bedroom,
not far from my bed,
just sitting on top of
the broken-down record player,
is
a wooden box
with a glass window
at the front.

In the box is Flora

and also Dora

You can't really tell who is Flora and who is Dora,
because they both have exactly the same
twitchy expression on their faces,
though I think Flora is just a little bit fatter.
(And a little bit foxier, too.)

What Flora and Dora like to do best of all
is to run very fast round and round inside a wheel.
Only for fun, though. Not like my dad who also
runs round and round in a circle as fast as he can,
(which isn't that fast).
Then he puffs.
You never hear Flora or Dora puff.
You only hear them squeaking on about
mouse things,
like pizza crumbs and how to hide in a toaster
if you see a cat.

Flora and Dora are very best friends.
Like me and my friend, Olive Higgie.
But you can easily tell the difference
between me and Olive Higgie
because she has black hair and she likes pickles,
but I don't.
Also, I can stand on my head and she can't,
but she can play Chopsticks on the piano.
Neither of us squeaks much,
unless someone tickles us.

One day, Olive Higgie comes over
to eat Cheezles and play.
We put the Cheezles on our fingers
and then we start throwing socks, and Olive Higgie,
who is trying to stand on her head,
accidentally bumps into the chair
and the chair accidentally falls over
and accidentally crashes into the box
on top of the broken-down record player
where Flora and Dora quite purposefully live.

OOPS says Olive Higgie,

and she puts her hand over her mouth.

Uh oh I say,

because there's a big hole in the glass.

The next day, Flora is gone.
She must have crawled out the hole,
looking for pizza crumbs or bits of cheesecake.
Or maybe she wanted to see the sleepy green field
where you can run round in big circles.
I look for her everywhere,
even inside Dad's woolly socks,
and behind the stove
where lots of old bits of spaghetti go.
But she isn't anywhere.

My dad fixes the hole so that Dora won't go.
But I am worried. I know it will be lonely for Dora
without her best friend Flora there.
Dora will have no one to share
special kinds of crumbs with.
No one to watch her run round the wheel
like a mighty champion.

Dad says,

Don't worry, mice don't get lonely

Olive Higgie and I take it in turns to hold Dora
very softly in the palms of our hands,
so she won't feel alone.
Dora stops running round in her wheel.
I guess she just doesn't feel like it any more.

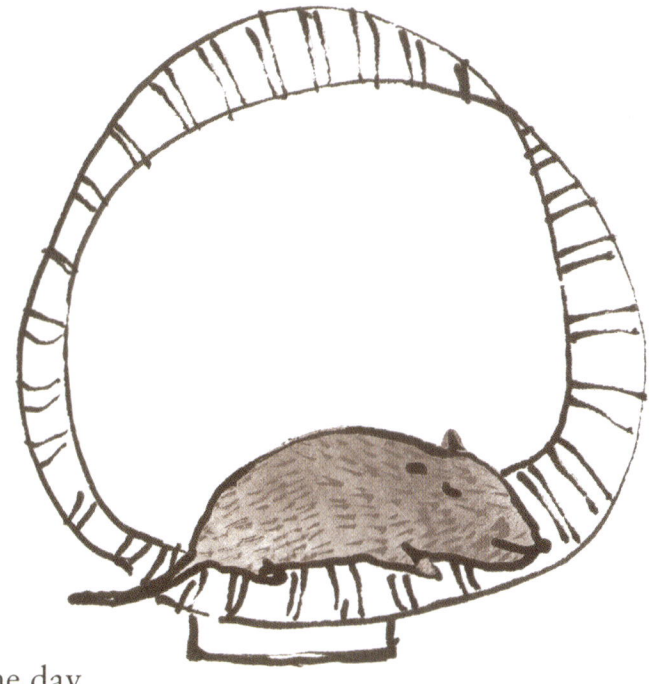

One day,
I find Dora lying completely still in the wheel.
I can tell she has died because of the way she looks.

'See,' I say to my dad. 'Dora has died of loneliness.'
And now he believes me that all things get lonely.

Even ants and beetles and cockroaches get lonely.

Even turtles, even squids and even sardines.

And my mum said especially doves, because they fall in love,

and especially dogs, like our dog Madge,

who always wants me to scratch her tummy.

Olive Higgie and I bury Dora near the daffodils,
and then we hold hands and close our eyes
and think good thoughts about Dora.

Olive Higgie says
she saw Flora sitting there, too,
but I'm not sure she really did.

The terrible terrible earthquake

One day, Olive Higgie says to me
that she has an Iggie in her bedroom.
And I say, 'What's an Iggie?'
And she says, 'An Iggie is a very good friend
of the Rietta who used to live on the Isle of Iggie,
but now lives with me because there was a terrible,
terrible earthquake on the Isle of Iggie.'
I say, 'Sheezamageeza!
A terrible earthquake on the Isle of Iggie.'
Then I say, 'What does an Iggie look like?'
And she does this drawing of an Iggie to show me,
and I say, 'That looks like a bandicoot.'
So she draws it again and I'm pleased to see
it doesn't have spots, since no one likes a copy cat.

And I say, 'What does an Iggie eat?'
And she says, 'Pickles and Cheezles.'
And I say, 'Oh my Lordy Lordy, pickles.'
I mean, who can seriously stomach pickles?
That poor old Iggie.
But Olive Higgie isn't worried. She says,
'Well, maybe the Rietta would like to meet the Iggie.'

And I say, 'Hmmm, yes, I think the Rietta would.'

So, next time I get in my bath
I speed off to the Island of the Rietta
and I go directly right past the
Wide Wide Long Cool Coast of the Lost Socks,

not even checking to see if either of my
long red socks with toes was having a visit,
and when I get to the island,
I am sorry to say
that things aren't in a good state there.
Oh Lordy Lordy, no they aren't.

For a start, the island has changed colour.
It isn't green any more, it's brown.
It looks like a bit of mud.
I fear that there's been a terrible terrible earthquake.
But that isn't what has happened.

'Good grief. You won't believe it,'
calls out the Puffed-up Pelican,
who knows everything and likes to gossip.
'What a disaster!'
'What happened?' I say.

'Good grief. You won't believe it,' says the Pelican, who can be repetitive when he's in the mood for spreading disaster stories.

'Oh please,
go ahead and tell me
what happened,' I say.
And the Pelican sighs,
'Well, if you must know,
the trees were all cut down.
Imagine!'
'Sheezamageeza!' I say.
'No trees!
Lordy Lordy, what a disaster.'

The Rietta is lying next to a rock.
It doesn't hoot.
It hardly raises its head.

A Rietta can't live without trees,
so I absolutely have to save it.
I rub its ears, like I do to Madge,
and then I take it to my bathtub,
and together we sail home.

On the way
the Rietta
eats the soap,
and bubbles
come out
its mouth.

I wrap the Rietta in a towel,
just like my mum does to me.
Then I give it some ice-cream. It hoots with joy.
All Riettas hoot when they're happy.

It likes to sleep in my bed, but it snores…

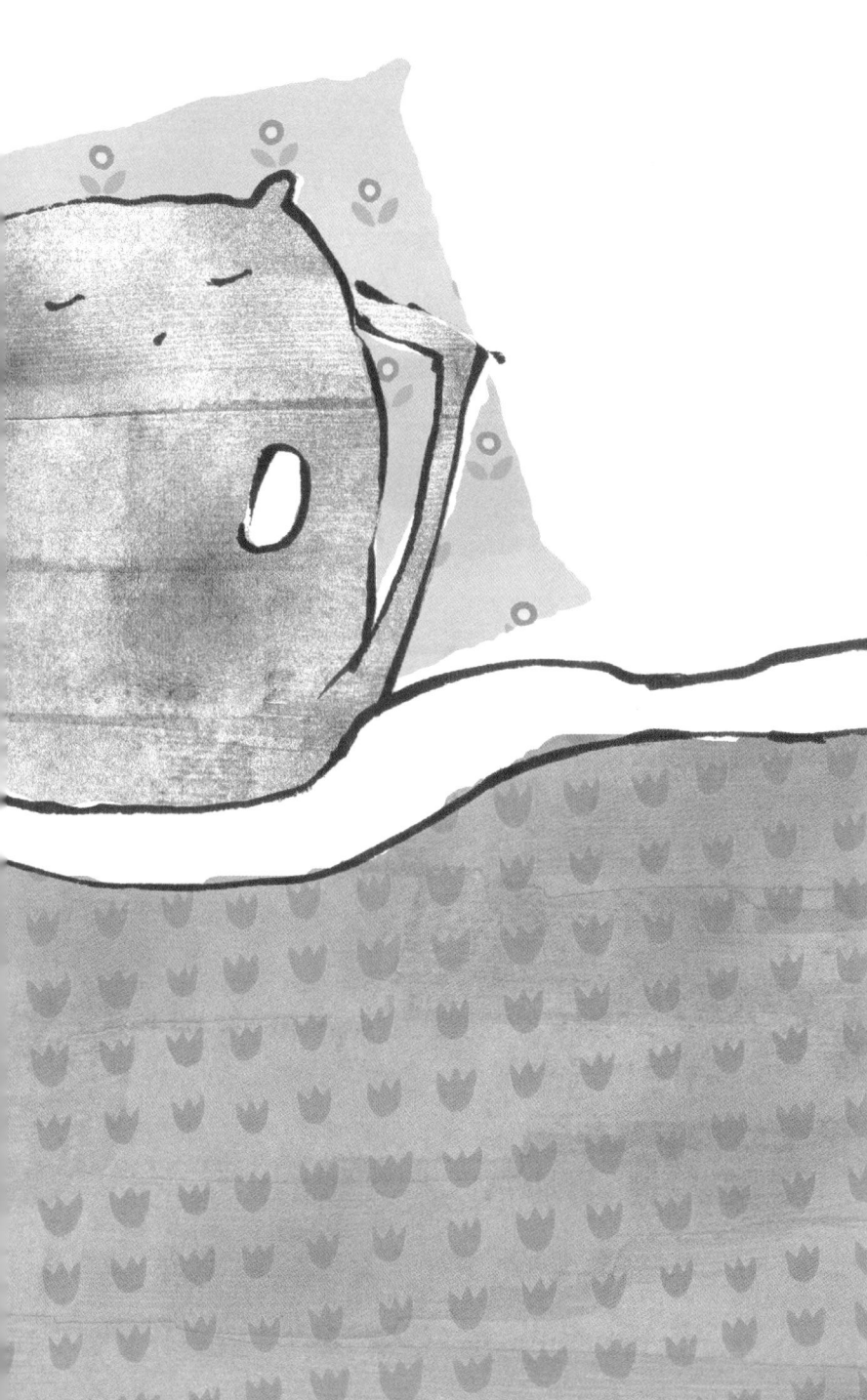

and its spots rub off on the sheets.

Sometimes we creep into the kitchen, while Mum is putting Albert to bed, and we eat a little more ice-cream straight from the tub.

It's the Rietta's **naughty nature** that makes me do it.

Other times, the Rietta looks out the window.
It just sits there and stares out
as if it has lost something in the night.
And that gets me thinking
about all the other lands out there,
because we need to find another land for the Rietta.
Like the

Land of the great untouched chocolate ripple

I tell the Rietta not to worry or feel sad,
because once it's bath time
we're going to do some more explorification.
We'll even take Albert with us,
because we could use an anchor man
and Albert is just the right size (sewing machine size)
to be an anchor,
just in case we need to stop and visit the Iggie
or rescue another Rietta,
because you just never know what will happen
once we get in that bath.

You never know!

Well, I'm Henrietta and little brother who only knows cleverer than Albert, my socks are know what stars are made of fed up, Albert's getting mucked with honey on my tummy. in a muddle, my socks are I like my long green socks with So I know what, I'll whip not the lot? Forget the It's really not so rude and gets a towel, says a flibberty I say, it's true be one too. socks no.

I've got long green socks with toes and a one word. fish. ⌇ I'm much older and much longer and my favourite colour's red. I and I don't want to go to bed. Mum's getting up, but I'm a grubby little sluggy I'm hoppy like a mossie and my mind's skew-whiff and my foot's in a puddle. toes, I don't want to get them wet. them off! It's getting hot, ☀ why frippery, I'll skindippery! to frolic in the nude. Mum sighs not to fidget, 'must you be gibbet?' I'm afraid I must, and when Albert grows up, he'll I'll give him my long green so he can do the 🧦🧦

frock-rocks

HENRIETTA
The Great Go-Getter

Henrietta P. Hoppenbeek would like to dedicate this book to Rico and Mannie, who accidentally landed on the Wide Wide Long Cool Coast of the Lost Socks and made a LOVELY hullabaloo there.

Hello everybody out there in the whirly old world.

It's me, Henrietta.

I'm the future Queen of the
Wide Wide Long Cool Coast
of the Lost Socks, so you'd better
listen to me because otherwise
I might have your head chopped off
and mashed up like potato and fed to the crocodiles.

Not really.

Everyone knows crocodiles don't like mash.

They like
a cup of peppermint tea
and a strawberry
cupcake.

And also, besides and on top of that, only very very nasty wicked queens will chop off your head, and actually I will be a very very perfectly nice queen who doesn't dribble one bit.

Lordy Lordy, you should see my brother Albert. He dribbles and dribbles, but he's only a baby so he can't help it. He can't help doing rude embarrassing things like

poo and **burps** and **growling**.

It's lucky I'm not a baby
because I DO like to be dignified,

> which means I poo in the loo
> and I walk like a queen
> and I eat ice-cream
> without putting
> it on my face.

I DO
like to be other things
as well.

For instance,
I'm very often
brave and **bold**,
and every now and then
I'm expOOperating
and expasperating
and ex**hill**perating.

106

If you don't know what that means ask your dad, because dads like to tell you stuff they know about.

Don't be fooled, though.

They might know a lot about golf or GERMAN PHILOSOPHERS or how to fix a broken thing, but dads don't know about Riettas or handstands,

and besides
and on top of that,
they've never been to the
Wide Wide Long Cool Coast
of the Lost Socks.

There's only one person in the whole whirly old world who can tell you about that, and that's

Henrietta the great go-getter.

So that's why you'd better listen.

There's
something going
on, and it isn't even
Christmas. I'll tell you what it
is. It's something in the house. It's a
D i l e m m a.
And if you don't know
what a Dilemma is,
don't worry because
I'll tell you now. A
Dilemma isn't quite a
first cousin of the
Dottypeejarma,
and it's only a very far
distant distant relation of the large dancing
Piggyleedrama, and, just in case you were
thinking it might be, a Dilemma isn't even a
creature at all, it's a PROBLEM. Like for
instance when you have a lost Rietta living in your
bedroom, which is exactly the problem I have.

Here's what a Dottypeejarma looks like.

Here's what a large dancing Piggyleedrama looks like.

You can see the Rietta is sadder than the others, and that's because it's lost. A Rietta is a particular kind of creature who helps you clown around, and Riettas are most definitely best when they're happy. They HOOT when they're happy. I like hooting. I like to hear it and I like to do it. But what I like to say best of all is Sheezamageeza. And when you have a Dilemma, you don't just say it as if you were saying, 'Oh dearie mearie, this is a bit of a pickle.' You say it with **oomph** and you say it with **poomph** like this...

Sheeza

What if you woke up next to a crocodile
rather than a Rietta?
Now that would be a BIG Dilemma.
Or what if your brother turned into a chocolate
ripple cake and you accidentally ate him because
you didn't hear him yelling out,
'It's me, Albert!'
That would also be a BIG BIG Dilemma.

Or what if you found that you
yourself had shrunk to the size
of a peanut, and Albert sat on you
because he didn't hear you calling out,
'Hey watch it, pudding!'
That would be what I call a DISASTER.
Because this is what I'd look like if Albert sat on me.

And if I was FLAT, how would I get in the bath
and sail to other lands?
As far as I know, flat people can't sail
because they probably just flap around
like wet towels in the wind.
And sail we must!
We absolutely have to find the Rietta a home
because the sadder the Rietta becomes
the more its spots fade.
Just this morning I noticed the Rietta's spots
were as pale as a tissue and I felt very very concerned.

I rang up Olive Higgie and I said, 'You won't believe it, but I think we have an EMERGENCY DILEMMA here.'

'Oh dearie mearie,' said Olive Higgie, who is my best friend and who has been known to eat pickles. 'Poor poor Rietta. What will we do?'

'Oh Lordy Lordy,' said I, Henrietta the great go-getter. 'Well, we'll get in the bath and we'll go find the Pelican on the rock and we'll ask him where can we find a home for the Rietta, because that Pelican is a busybody who knows exactly precisely who is who and which is what and how a dot and why the plot and what the…'

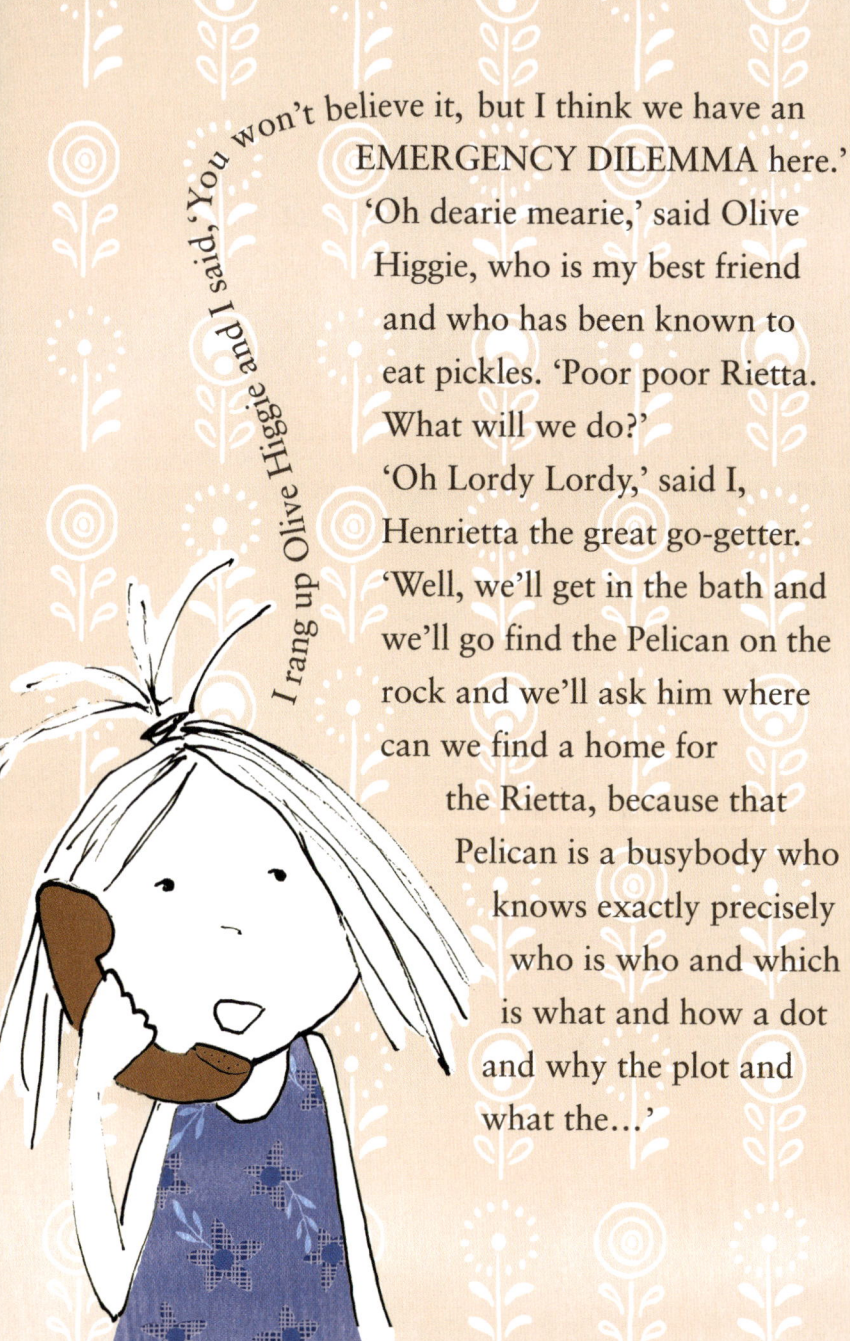

'Busybody? What's a busybody?' said Olive Higgie. 'A busybody,' said I, pretending not to notice that Olive Higgie had interrupted my poem, 'a busybody is someone who stands on a rock and watches all the goings on around him and tells anyone anything and forgets to do his exercises or write his own poems and often wears a red raincoat so that you don't mistake him for a mushroom or a lighthouse.'
'Oh,' said Olive Higgie.
'When do we leave?' And I said, 'Bathtime of course.'

Sheezamageeza, there's another Dilemma.
A Bathtime Dilemma. Guess who's in the bath?
Albert. Little pudding. He makes me laugh.
'Listen Albert, we've got serious business,' I say,
and he just smiles at me and I give him
a quick squidge, which is the kind of squeeze
you give someone you accidentally love.
'Okay little pumpkin,' I say, because that's what
Mum calls him, even though he doesn't look
one bit like a pumpkin because he's not orange.
'Okay little muffin,' I say, because that's also
what Mum calls him and I like muffins better
than pumpkins.

'Looks like you'll just have to come along
'cause we absolutely have to go and do some
serious **explorification**.'

Albert blows a raspberry.

'For the sake of the Rietta,' I add in a hushed
voice, just so Mum can't hear, because she
doesn't know about the Rietta.

Albert holds up the soap and says, **'fish?'**

And I begin to wonder...

If Albert thinks the soap is a fish,

and Mum thinks Albert is a pumpkin,

and Olive thinks pickles are yummy,

then anything can be anything...

A bath can be a boat,

and a muffin can be a cushion,

and a pickle can wear a hat,

and a pea can be grumpier than a grown-up,

and the fading dots can cover the darkening sky and…

and the great

Henrietta can learn to fly.

Not really. Everyone knows
you have to eat lots of
brussel sprouts if you
want to learn to fly,
and I don't like
b r u s s e l
sprouts.
N o t
one
bit.

So we'll have to sail after all.

I get in the bath with Albert

and the Rietta,

and we stop by to pick up Olive Higgie.
I whisper, 'This time we won't drop Albert
off in the Land of One Thousand Alberts
because we might just need him.'
Olive Higgie says, 'How could we possibly
need Albert? He can't even walk yet.'
'As an anchor, of course.'
Olive Higgie thinks a bit and then says,
'Okay, giddy-up,' because she's a bit excited
and has mistaken the bath for a horse.
Albert says, 'boat?' And the Rietta gives a little
hopeful HOOT and then we set sail
to find the Pelican.

The Pelican

The Pelican has his back to us,
so when we get close to his rock
I yell out and he jumps up and squawks,
'Good grief, good grief. Why must all little children yell? It makes me feel jumpy and I only have a small rock and if I jump I might land on the wrong side of the rock and I try never never to land on the wrong side of the rock.'
'Why?' I ask.
'Good grief. There you go. All little children ask "Why?" Another most annoying habit. Especially when there's no answer. Some things are just done one way and not the other. Like when you eat toast you put butter on one side and not the other. Now how would you feel if some noisy yelling pelican came along and asked you, "Why? Why do you put your butter on that particular side of the toast and not on the other particular side of the toast?" Actually, come to think about it, why don't you put butter on both sides? Hmmm?'

We all think about this for a minute. I have to admit it, that know-all squawker Pelican has a point. Before I can come up with an idea, which is what I usually do, he goes and squawks again,
'Good grief, what on earth are you doing with a **lost** Rietta on board?'
'It's losing its spots,' says Olive Higgie.
'Of course it is. All Riettas lose their spots when they're lost. Their spots don't like sad skin so they start to leave, and once a Rietta has lost its spots it isn't a Rietta any more.'
'Oh dearie mearie,' says Olive Higgie. The Rietta makes a sad little noise and tilts its head to the side, and I give it a reassuring rub on its back where it especially likes to be rubbed. Riettas are very very sensitive and Pelicans aren't one bit sensitive.

'What does a Rietta become once it loses its spots?'
I say.
'A pale shadow of its former self,' pronounces
the Pelican.
'What's that?' says Olive Higgie.
'It's a Moonbeam,' says the Pelican,
who holds out his wings for dramatic effect.
'Oh Lordy Lordy.'
'And further furthermore,' says the Pelican,
with an extra dramatic dip of his beak,
'you may wonder what indeed happens to the spots
when the Rietta loses them.'
'Do they become stars in the sky?' says Olive Higgie
hopefully, because she's a dreamy girl.

'I'm afraid not,' snorts the Pelican. 'The spots look for some happy skin. They look for frinkles and they look for squidges and for gurgles and for dribbles, for these are all signs of happiness, and the spots live off happiness.'

'What's a frinkle?' I ask.

The Pelican puffs himself up because if there's one thing a busybody pelican likes it's to know things that other people don't know.

'A frinkle is a fat wrinkle, of course.'

'Well, I'm not fat so those spots aren't going to land on me,' I say.

'Me neither,' says Olive Higgie, and then we both look at Albert who opens his mouth to laugh and

Sheezamageeza!

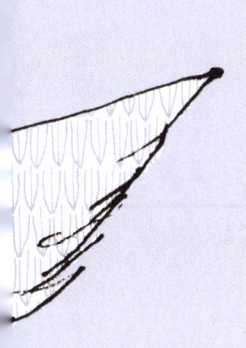

He's covered in spots. Pale blotchy spotty spots.
'Albert?' I gasp. 'Are you all right?'
Albert gurgles and dribbles
and makes a **grrrr** sound.
'Of course he's all right. He's happy as Larry.
That's why the spots are landing on him.
And if you don't get rid of those spots
he'll soon turn into a Rietta himself!'

Olive Higgie says, 'Who's Larry?' and I say,
'Don't worry about Larry. Oh Lordy Lordy, look,
now Albert really does look like a muffin. A smiling
gurgling sultana muffin.'
And the Rietta, well the Rietta is staring out to sea,
looking pale and thin as a sheet. I'm afraid to say it
but the Rietta is losing its frinkles.
'Oh Lordy Lordy, what shall we do?' I say.
'Poor poor Rietta. And poor poor poor Albert.'
'And poor poor spots,' says Olive Higgie,
because Olive Higgie is an arty girl who likes
spots and stripes and triangles and stars.

'I'll tell you what you'd better do,' declares the
Pelican, and his wings elbow the air out of his way
as he leans towards us. 'You better get to the
Wide Wide Long Cool Coast of the Lost Socks
very quick sticks. I've heard a rumour that there
just might be a small colony of Riettas living there!'

The Wide Wide Long Cool Coast of the Lost Socks

We sail as fast as a bath can sail directly towards the Wide Wide Long Cool Coast of the Lost Socks. We can see the lost socks lounging under the palm trees, sunbaking and relaxing and no doubt having some thoughts as well. Olive Higgie suddenly looks a bit afraid and she says, 'Henrietta, have you ever met a lost sock?' 'Not yet.' 'Well then how do we know the lost socks aren't nasty or cruel or very very bad?' I think about this for a minute, and since it's my job to be bold I say, 'When you're doing serious emergency explorification, then you have to be brave and hope for the best, but at the same time be prepared for the worst, which means we leave Albert on the shore, tied to the bath, so the bath won't float away. If the socks are nasty we can jump back in the bath and sail away on a cheerful breeze.'

Olive Higgie looks at Albert and then at me and then at the Rietta and then she nods her head and says, 'Okay, onwards brave soldiers,' because she's a bit afraid and has mistaken the Wide Wide Long Cool Coast for a battlefield.

So we tie Albert to the bath and leave him playing with a rubber duck. Then Olive Higgie and I and the Rietta creep up quietly towards the lost sock sunbaking area.

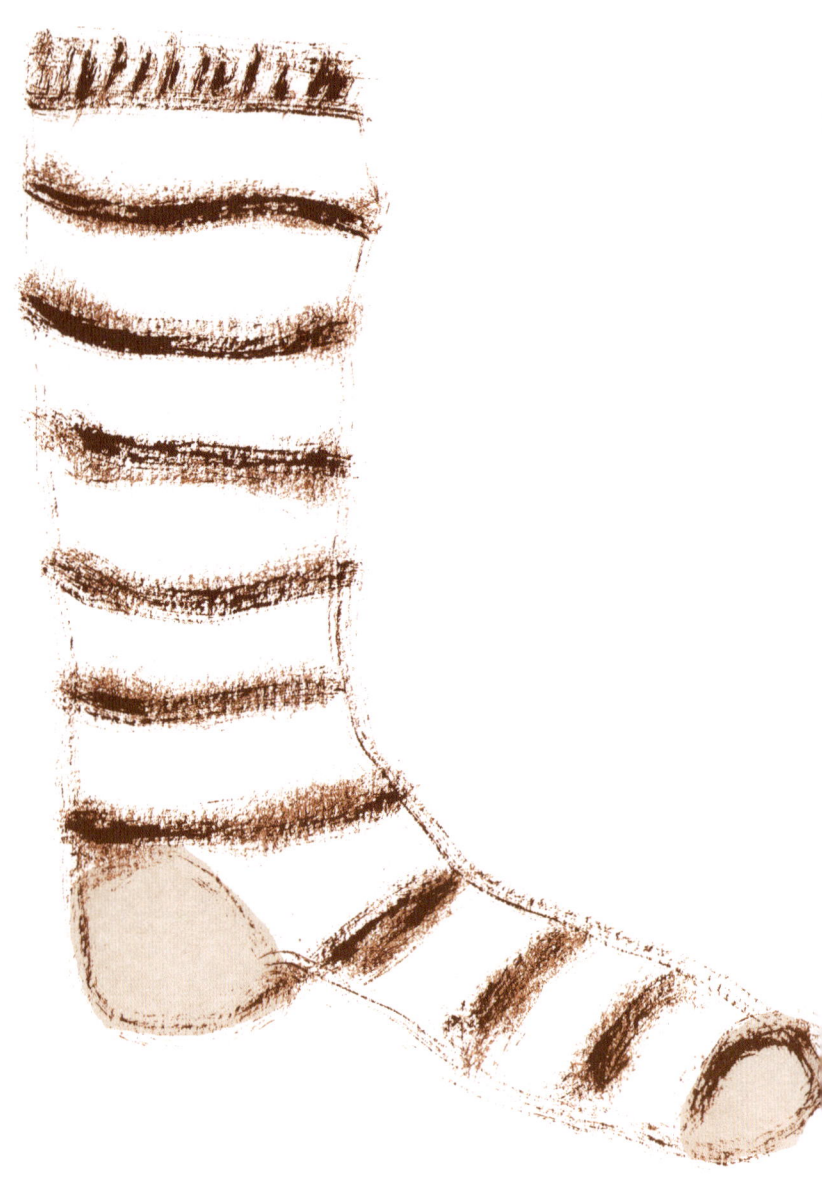

A long striped sock notices us first. He slowly wriggles up on his heel and says, 'Hey guys, are you lost?'
'No, no we're not lost, we're looking for the Rietta colony.'
'Dudes, if you're not lost then we can't let you on the island. Only lost socks, lost slobs and lost souls are allowed here. And that means no tourists, no superheroes and no astronauts.'

'What's a dude?' whispers Olive Higgie to me,
and I whisper back that I suspect it might be
a person who comes from the town of Dudelings,
where they mainly say rude things, but I'm not
absolutely sure. Then I turn to the sock.
'We've got a Dilemma,' I declare, since future
queens are allowed to make declarations,
especially when the Rietta is getting paler by the
minute, which means that Albert is probably getting
fatter and starting to HOOT.
'A Dilemma?' says
Long Striped Sock.
'I never heard of a Dilemma.
Do we allow Dilemmas?'
'Only if they can sew,'
says a tattered looking
sock with holes.
Then I say in a loud
important voice,

'Excuse me but we're in a big hurry to find
this sad fading Rietta a home, because it's lost.'

'

screeches a smart black business sock.
'Why didn't you say that in the first place?'
And then all the socks pop up and hop over
and roll around the Rietta saying,
'Welcome to the club.'
And indeed the Rietta manages to HOOT,
because there's nothing a Rietta loves more
than being the centre of a hullabaloo.

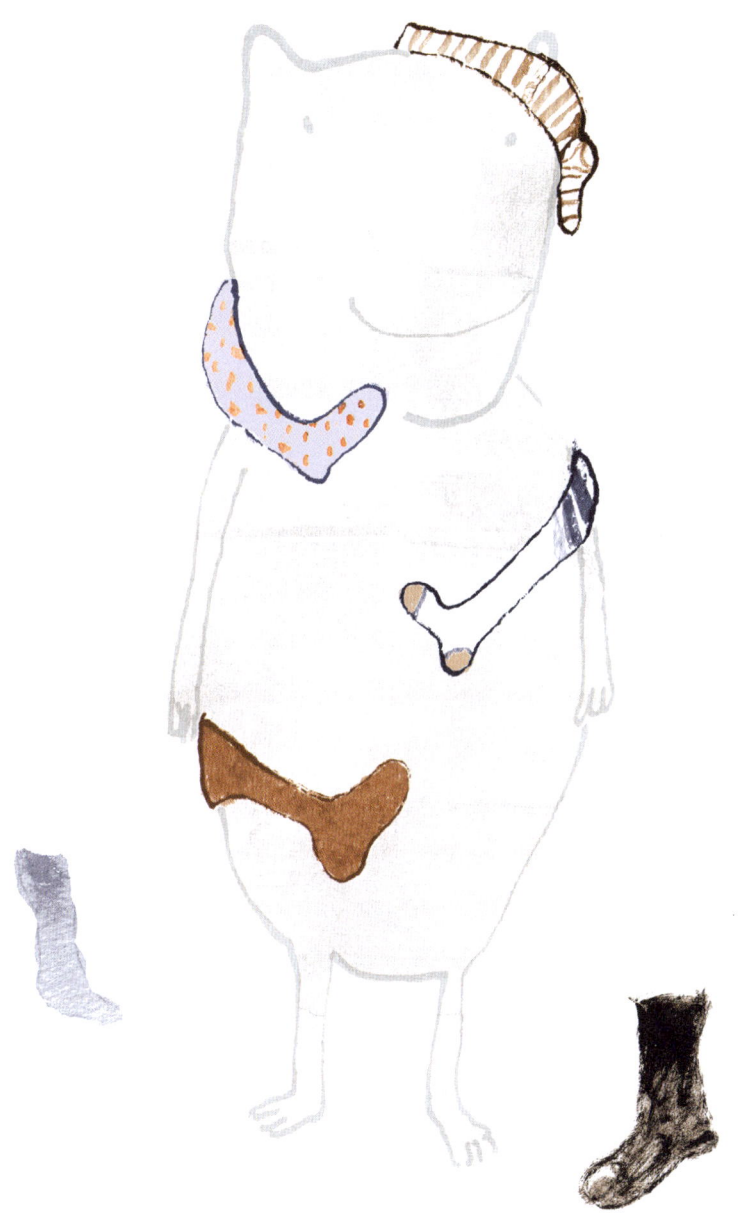

'He-hmmm,' I say, which is exactly the right thing to say when the attention is no longer on you and it absolutely should return to you. 'Excuse me, Lost Socks, but we have an EMERGENCY DILEMMA because we need to find a home for this Rietta V.Q.S. (which, in case you don't know, stands for Very Quick Sticks) or it will become a Moonbeam!'

Long Striped Sock says, 'Cool, a Moonbeam!'

Tattered Holey Sock says, 'Poor sod.'

Smart Black Business Sock says, 'Emergency Dilemmas are not allowed and Moonbeams are against the law, unless they are very smelly indeed.'

And just as I'm beginning to despair, a bouncy little tennis sock sidles up to me and whispers,

'I've got an idea, but you have to follow me.'

I have a consultation with Olive Higgie, since she is second mate.

'Would you trust a tennis sock?' I say.

And she has a quick think and says, 'If you would.'

So I have an even quicker think, and since I'm a very very quick thinker I don't even have time to hear my thoughts think before I say, 'Okay we'll follow.'

Because, let's face it, we don't have any choice but to trust a tennis sock.

Farewell O.H.

First of all we go over a big sand dune and then we slide down the other side and come to a jungle. There's a sign which says:

> Beware
> The Bungry
> jungle

'Oh dearie mearie,' says Olive Higgie.
'Oh Lordy Lordy,' says I, because everyone knows that there's nothing as hungry as a bungry.

Bungries eat anything,
you name it:
roast pork, roast unicorn,
roast great-aunt-susan,
even peas, beans and salad greens,
even brussels sprouts and pickles,
and probably your rubbish and your dirty washing,
and most probably your local dentist
and the prime minister,
though no one knows for sure.
But I know one thing for sure,
a bungry would love to eat
little girl explorers.

Bouncy Little Tennis Sock jumps up and down in an excited way,
which isn't very reassuring,
and Olive Higgie says,
'Perhaps I should go back and mind Albert?'
which is really an excellent idea.
I wish I'd thought of that myself,
but someone has to stay behind
and lead the explorification onwards.

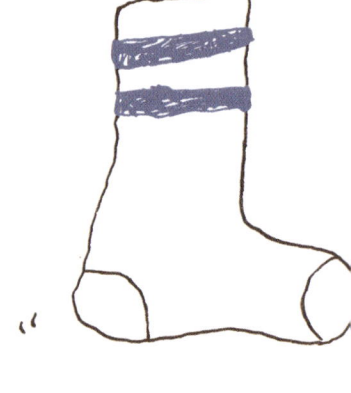

'Farewell O.H.,' I say with a sniff.
O. H., in case you didn't notice,
is code name for Olive Higgie,
and code names
should always be used
when the explorification
has reached a possibly tragic
and important climax.
I watch O.H.
scuttle back V.Q.S.
to find Albert, and,
to tell you the truth,
I begin to feel a bit lonely.
But the Rietta rubs up
against me because
it knows I'm about to be
VERY BRAVE indeed.

'Ready?' says Tennis Sock, with an eager leap.
'Aren't you one bit afraid of being eaten?' I say,
since it's not every day you meet a fearless tennis
sock, so I'm curious.

'Bungries don't eat socks.'

'Oh I see. Well, lucky for you you're a sock
and not a person like me. What about
Riettas? Do bungries eat them?'
We both look at the Rietta,
who is now only a faint outline,
and the sock says, with a heartless giggle,
'They won't eat this one.
Nothing left to eat!'
I have a bit of an emergency ponder.
If bungries don't eat socks then I
might just disguise myself as a sock.
A blue spotty sock in fact,
since that is my very favourite kind.

I tell the sock my plan and it laughs and jumps
and says, 'Yes, what a joke. Good idea.'
Luckily there happens to be
an old leftover Christmas stocking
hanging from a Christmas tree,
and it's just exactly my size.

So I wr^{i}gg$_l$e in and off we hop,
the tennis sock and I,
with the Rietta pattering along beside us.

The Bungry Jungle

Inside the sock,

in the deep deep depths
of the Bungry Jungle…

I can hear my heart going
thud thud thud very very loudly.
And I wonder if real socks have hearts,
and if a bungry just happened to hear
a heart inside a sock, would it be suspicious?
I try very hard to make my heart quiet,
but the harder I try
the louder it thumps
and the louder it thumps
the more scared I become
and the more scared I become
the louder it thumps
and the louder it thumps
the harder I have to try to stop it thumping,
which isn't working at all
because then,
quite suddenly...

there is a real live long hungry bungry nose
and it is sniff sniff sniffing,
and a suspicious bungry ear
listen listen listening
to my heart thud thud thudding,
and then, oh Lordy Lordy,
a bungry mouth open open opening and...

The bungry sneezes because the Rietta is tickling its nose and acting like a spooky ghost, and the bungry is scuttling back into the trees like a little scaredy cat.

PHEW.

The tennis sock
is laughing its heel off.
'What's so funny?' I ask
in the manner of a queen.
'I nearly got eaten.'
'Ha ha,' it says. 'Exactly!
What a hilarious joke I played.
See, everybody thinks
bungries will eat anything,
but there's a **Big** Secret
only lost socks know.'

'What's the secret?' I say,
because if there's one thing I love
it's discovering a Big Secret.
'Shhh,' says the sock.
Then it whispers,
'Do you know why
there's nothing
as hungry as a bungry?
Because bungries don't
eat anything except air.
Bungries don't really
eat people
or socks
or steaks
or anything.
They're AIR-ARIANS.'

Well I've heard of vegetarians, because that's
what my mum is, and my dad says he'd like to be
a roast lamb-arian, which means I might just as well
be a chocolate ripple cake-arian, but I've never
heard of an air-arian. I don't think I'd like
to be one of those.

Tennis Sock is still roaring with laughter.
'Yes, clouds for lunch, sunset for dinner and
blue skies for dessert. Ha ha, and you even dressed
up as a sock. Lucky you didn't dress up as a cloud.
Ha ha. Wait till I tell the others. Do excuse me
for making a joke at your expense, but it's so boring
down there on the shore. Too sunny and relaxing.
I do have to amuse myself somehow. Tennis socks
need a bit of a bounce.'

'Hmmph,' I say, which is exactly the thing to say
when a lost tennis sock has made you look
like a fool and you only half forgive them,
though there's a chance that if they are especially
nice to you, like if they read you a story or make
you laugh, then you will forgive them completely.

The Gel Site W.

There's no time for sulking because
the Rietta looks too tired to go much further.
So I get ready to keep going, but Tennis Sock
points us towards a dark tunnel.
'This is where I leave you, I'm afraid. You have to
pass through this tunnel. On the other side is the
Wide Wide Coast of the Woolly Wanderers.
But no sock has ever come out of that tunnel,
so no sock should go in.'
There's a sign in front of the tunnel:
Gel Site W. No body welcome.
'What does that mean?' I ask.
'No one knows,'
says Tennis Sock,
'but if you find out,
do tell me. Cheerio.'
The mischievous sock bounces away
and I think to myself that if a tennis
sock has a heart it is a small heart
that ticks like an alarm clock.

The Rietta and I
look at the tunnel.
'Well, Gel sounds like jelly,
so maybe it's nice and soft
and squishy in there,' I say
in a hopeful way, but the Rietta
doesn't believe me, and nor do I,
because, let's face it, this tunnel
isn't exactly looking like a fun palace.
It's dark and hollow and cold, and worst of all
there's a very stinky smell coming out.
The Rietta lies down and I realise it can't
go any further, which means that I'm the only one
left on the expedition. It's all up to me.
Henrietta the great go-getter.
I sigh loudly and pat the
Rietta and I say,
'Don't worry,
I'll save you.'
Then I close my eyes
and plunge bravely into the tunnel.

As soon as I enter, I hear a loud booming voice.

who's there?

I can't see anyone but I smell someone, and,
I can tell you, whoever or whatever it is in there,
it really pongs.
'It's just me, Henrietta, and I'm only a small girl
who is passing through on my way to find
a Rietta colony. Sorry to bother you. I would have
knocked but there wasn't a knocker.'

'No body is welcome in here. And I don't like small
girls,' says the angry voice.
'Oh dear, well, let me see. Do you like explorers?'
'I don't like no body and no body likes me
and you better not come any closer.'
'Why not?' I say boldly, because everyone knows
you shouldn't annoy someone who smells revolting
and seems a lot bigger than you.
'Because I am a monster and
I will chomp you with my rotting teeth
and stomp on you with my huge feet
and breathe on you with my foulest breath
and dribble on you with my disgusting spit...'
'Dribble? Hmmph, that's nothing. I'm used to that.
I bet you don't dribble as much as my brother
Albert.'
'What? What did you say?' yells the monster,
and then he steps forward out of the dark.

When I see him, can you imagine what I say?

sheezamageeza

And I say it with oomph
and I say it with poomph.
And then I say, in the manner of a queen
'Excuse me but you forgot to get dressed
because he's only wearing his
underpants and two odd socks.

'Well I wasn't expecting a visitor,' he says. And then he roars, 'Now **you** listen here, young lady. I've got goobies in my nose holes and mouldies in my toenails. I've got yucky stuff between my teeth

and
yellow stuff
in my ears.
I've got fluff
in my
belly button,
and hairs
on my
fatty bottom.
I've got
gooey gums
and pongy
breath and
grizzly plans
and sweaty
hands,
and no body,
I say
NO BODY,
can
beat that!'

'Albert can.'
'No he can't,' roars the monster.
'Do you poo your pants?'
'Of course I don't. That's DISGUSTING!'
'Well Albert does.'
'What?' he roars. 'You're making me very angry. This Albert is making me very angry. I'm afraid I'll have to take you for a prisoner and stuff you in my pillow with all the other lost socks. Unless, of course… well, there's only one way to save yourself now and that's to tell me what Gel Site W. stands for.'

Don't **you** know?' Of course I know. But I've forgotten. I live in a dark tunnel. I don't eat any vegetables. I can't think straight and I can't think curly, I can't think at all. So if you can think it for me, I'll let you go.'

'Fair enough,' I say, which is exactly what you should say when a monster is making a deal with you. I try to think. I try thinking straight and I try thinking curly, but the only thought I can think is that I might just be stuffed in a pillow and never heard of again. Just when I'm about to give up, I hear a familiar cry coming from far away.

Boy am I happy to hear that. It's dear old O.H., and there she is on the other side of the tunnel, on the coast which is known as the Wide Wide Coast of the Woolly Wanderers. She's in the sea with Albert, bobbing up and down in the bathtub, and they're waving at me. And then O.H. is getting out of the bath and jumping, in a heroic fashion, onto the shore and hurrying V.Q.S. towards me. When she sees the monster, she stops and puts her hands on her hips and she says,

'Well, you must be the Greatest Ever Living Slob In The Entire World!'

And then the monster howls and roars and
stamps his ugly feet and moans
and I say, 'There there, she didn't mean it.'
And he says, 'Yes she did. She guessed it.

Gel Site W. That's what it stands for.

Greatest **E**ver **L**iving **S**lob **I**n **T**he **E**ntire **W**orld.

See, I'm not really a monster. I'm only a slob.'
'You're the Greatest Slob though. That's something,'
says O.H.
'What about Albert?' says the Greatest Slob.
'He poos his pants.'
At that moment O.H. and I both look at each other
because we remember that we've forgotten Albert
and the Rietta.
Olive Higgie says, 'Wait here, I'll get Albert.'
And I say, 'Wait here too, I'll get the Rietta.'
And the Greatest Slob starts to dribble.

Albert Saves the Day

When I return with the poor faded
Rietta, Olive Higgie is there with Albert
and something else as well.
'Look H.P.,' she says proudly.
'Look what Albert found.
When I got back to the bath
there was Albert, and he was
playing with a baby Rietta.'
Sure enough, there is a little spotty
grinning gurgling baby Rietta,
and when my big Rietta sees that baby
it begins to make a funny noise
like a pigeon. It takes the baby
in its paws and rocks it,
and a big tear rolls down its face
and it looks at me and HOOTS.
And I can't help it,
because I'm so happy
a big tear rolls
down my face.

Then I look at O.H. and Albert, because at times
like these you need your brother or your friend
or your sister or your dad to be by your side,
even for a moment, just in case all your big feelings
make you wobble or jump or explode.
But, Lordy Lordy, Albert is being picked up
by the Greatest Slob, and Albert isn't one bit scared
or disgusted. He just gives the Slob a big squidge,
because Albert loves everybody,
even if they are a slob.
And now the Greatest Slob is weeping.
'No one has ever cuddled me before.'

'Oh dear, that's very bad. Everyone needs
a cuddle and a squidge,' I say. 'But I'm afraid
you can't keep Albert because he's my baby brother
and I happen to like having him around,
and my mum and dad are quite mad about him too,
and we all like to get on the bed together and
have a bit of a roll and a giggle in the mornings.'
'What you need,' says O.H., 'is one of those
woolly wanderers out there to keep you company.
I happen to know that there is one in particular

who has just lost its friend.'
She points at one sitting out on the beach,
and the Greatest Slob puts Albert down
and walks over to the woolly wanderer.
O.H. is a very clever girl, and I'm feeling a little
jealous that she has come up with such
a fine idea which will possibly save us all.
She whispers to me, 'That woolly wanderer is
the one who has been looking after the baby Rietta,
so the poor thing is lonely.'

'Good thinking, O.H.,' I say
because you have to
admit it when
someone else
on the team has
a good thought,
and then
I try to have
an equally
good thought,
but not
a better one,
just an equal one.
'Otherwise,' I say,
'I would
have to

take the woolly wanderer
home with me and
    it would probably
        eat all the ice-cream
      and leave
        dirty marks
          on my sheets.'
          'Good thinking
            H.P.,' says O.H.
          and then we
          both feel
            very satisfied
           and very
              EQUALLY
            clever
              together.

We watch the Greatest Slob and the lonely woolly wanderer say hello. The big Rietta and the baby Rietta begin to HOOT together, and you can see that the Rietta is becoming all fat and spotty again from the togetherness.

Then Albert starts to rub his eyes and that means we'd better jump in that bathtub and get him home, because if there's one thing that's almost as good as bathtime, it's bedtime, when Dad reads us a story about all the amazing things that can happen…

I give the Rietta a big squidge,
and the Rietta gives me a big squidge,
and even though it won't be living
in my bedroom, I know that whenever
I need to make a hullabaloo and have a
HOOT, I can just remember the Rietta
and know that it's making a hullabaloo
and having a HOOT too. And in some
way we will always be together.

HENRIETTA

Gets a Letter

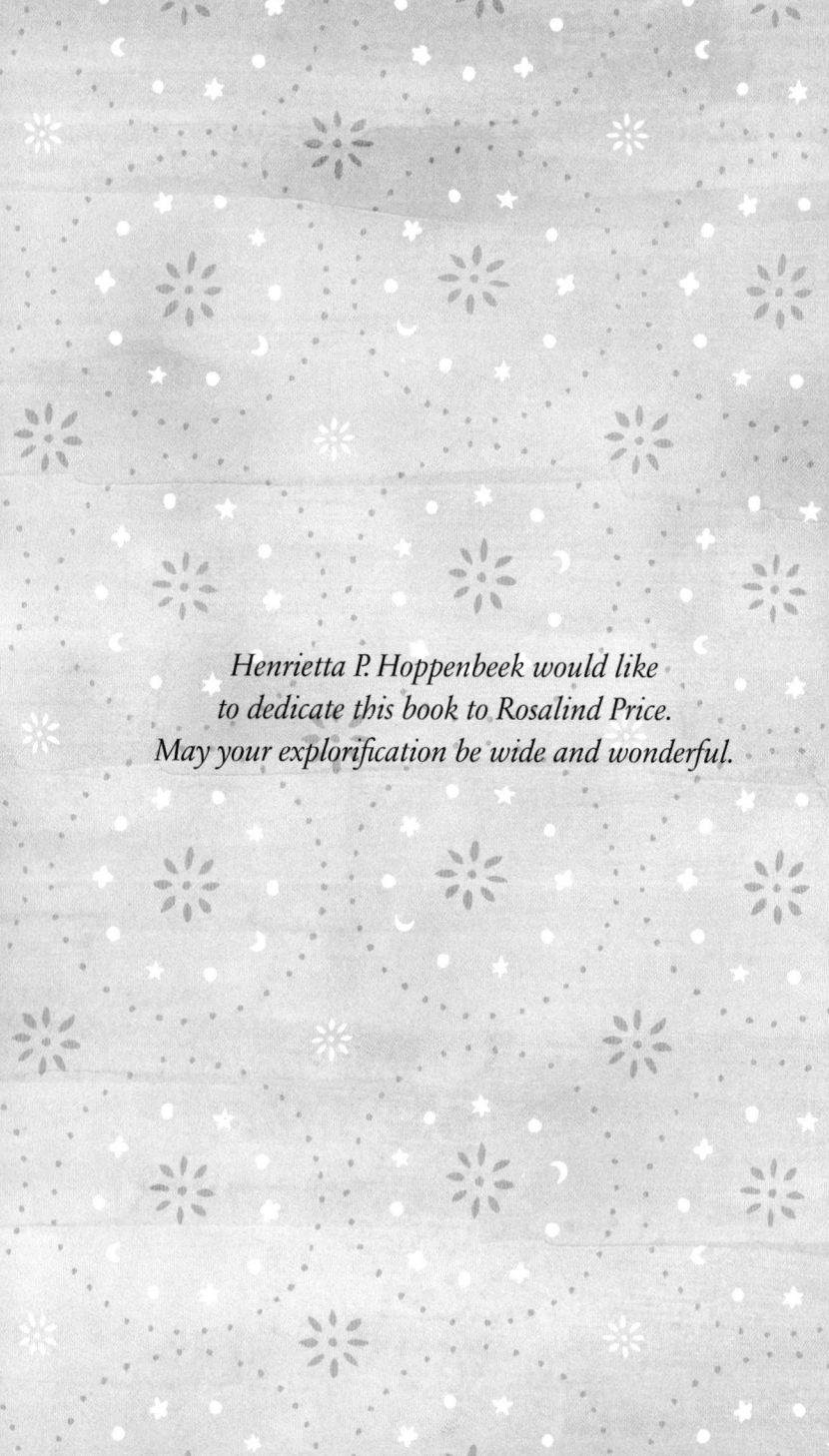

*Henrietta P. Hoppenbeek would like
to dedicate this book to Rosalind Price.
May your explorification be wide and wonderful.*

This is me. I'm Henrietta.

Dad says there's no one better, but that's because he loves me. Kings and queens and angels probably are better.

Also, animals who don't bite are very good. I don't bite, not unless you happen to be a chocolate ripple cake.

Here's Albert. He's my brother and he hasn't learnt to poo in the loo yet.

Here is Mum and Dad,

and Madge, our fat brown dog,

and Grannie who wears gumboots, and Grampa who gives prickly kisses

and
Olive Higgie,
my best friend,

and
cousin Edgar
who draws
pictures
of cars,

and Aunt Lulu
who was once
in a circus.

Uncle George is meant to be here but Mum says,
'No doubt he has slept in.'

Uncle George is a scallywag, which means
he is sometimes getting into trouble.

We're having a party for Albert because he is two.

Here's the birthday cake.
Lordy Lordy, it's chocolate ripple cake.
I can hardly stop myself from biting it.
Everybody sings Happy Birthday Albert.
Lucky Albert.
Everybody has a piece of cake except Madge,
because she's a greedy-guts with a fat tummy.

Albert's piece is bigger than mine.
I'm absolutely sure it is.
'That's not fair!' I say loudly,
because it's important to let everyone know
when there has been an injustice.
'Albert's piece is bigger than mine!'
'That's because it's his birthday,' says Mum.
Dad says,
'You'll get the biggest piece on your birthday.'
Aunt Lulu says,
'Don't worry, too much cake will give you spots.'
Olive Higgie looks alarmed,
but Grannie pats her on the wrist and says,
'Lulu is just teasing.'
I'm cross.

Very, very cross. I can't wait till it's *my* birthday.

Albert has smeared his BIG piece of cake all over his face. And he has a new train.

I can't bear it. I fold my arms and sink into a huff. No one notices. Then I frown as hard as I can. Still no one notices. Then I snort and kick the table leg about fifty times.

Mum says, 'Henrietta, please stop kicking the table, it's driving me mad.'

So I stomp off to my room, slam the door, throw myself on the bed and wail.

No one comes. Not even Olive Higgie, my best friend. I stop wailing because I'm too busy thinking how unfair it is that I'm stuck in my room missing out on the party when everyone else is having a nice time without me.

The more I think about it, the crosser I get, and the crosser I get, the more I think there is only one thing left to do.

I explode into fifty billion pieces of Henrietta.

Not really. I try very hard to explode but nothing happens except a slight ache in my head. So I lie on the floor next to my corduroy donkey and give up on being cross. I try to think of things like outer space and puppies, and then I hear a

STRANGE and OMINOUS

scuffling noise under my bed. What could it be? Before I have time to investigate, Uncle George bursts into my room wearing a hat and singing, 'Don't let me be lonely, come dance with me, oh dance with me...'

'Uncle George, you're very late and you missed out on cake.'

'Good. I don't care for cake.'

And I say,
'Well, neither do I, actually.'

And he says,
'Oh really? How very grown up. So what do you care for?'

'Lots of things. For instance, Olive Higgie, and my dog Madge, but today I don't particularly care for Albert.'

And he says,
'Well, I care very much for the lovely Miss Lily Fantuzzi, the local librarian.'

I roll my eyes at this.

Then he says, 'I like to wear a hat, for no reason,
and to give something to someone else,
even a small thing.'
And I say, 'Me too.
I do drawings for Grannie.
She sticks them on her fridge.'
And he says,
'Well, I particularly like
to dance at a party.'
'Me too.'
'Oh, but I like to dance
with a good dancing partner.'
And I say, 'Me too,
only the very very finest.'
And then he takes me by the hand,
as if I were a ballerina,
and we go into the lounge room
and he bows and takes off his hat.
'Can we please have some music?
Henrietta and I would very much care to dance.'

We look very swish because Uncle George is always dancing with the ladies, so he knows all the moves.

And I forget all about the cake and getting cross because there are much better things to care about.

Like cuddles with Mum, for example.

And also investigating

STRANGE and OMINOUS noises...

Under the bed

Now it's night-time and the moon is out. I'm meant to be in bed, but I'm sitting on the floor having serious thoughts. Serious thoughts sometimes make you feel bad, whereas splendid thoughts always make you feel good. But sometimes there are serious thoughts that just have to be thought about – there's no way around or over or under it.

For instance, I absolutely cannot get into bed until I work out what made that

OMINOUS and STRANGE noise I heard.

I don't think it's a crocodile, because crocodiles like to sit up and have tea and strawberry cupcakes. They don't want to slob around under a bed.

I don't think it could be a rhino, because rhinos prefer to point their horns in a threatening manner.

And if it was an elephant, the bed would look like this:

squashed

It might just be a monster, but I've heard that monsters lurk around in dark misty lakes eating dark misty lake bugs. So it's unlikely to be a monster. Very unlikely.

What *is* under my bed?

It might just be the kind of thing that likes to bite little girls' legs. And if it is, Dad should have a look under the bed, because you can't be a biter of dad legs *and* little girl legs. That's two different things.

'Dad!'

Dad pokes his head in the door.

'There's a scruffly something under my bed.'

So Dad slouches down under the bed. 'Have a good look Dad. It could be hiding.'

'I see one red crayon, one striped sock, a pair of pyjama pants, a corduroy donkey and a piece of Lego,

but there's not one single monster under this bed. Anyway, monsters are vegetarian,' he says.

'I know that. They only eat spinach and dark misty lake bugs, if you really want to know.'

Dad says, 'Is that so? I bet they'd prefer Albert's last piece of chocolate ripple cake!' And he growls like a monster and pretends to eat my foot.

After Dad tucks me in, I have a wandering kind of a think about monsters and cake. If the monster under my bed has plodded over hills and valleys to eat the last piece of chocolate ripple cake, and it doesn't get it, that monster could be very grumpy and very hungry. I immediately dash into the kitchen to get that last piece of cake. I take two tiny nibbles, just to check it still tastes good. Then I put it on a plate, poke it under my bed and do a spectacular, monster-avoiding leap onto my bed.
I snuggle down and lie very still so I can hear the monster when it starts to scuffle about.

The pickle trap

When I wake up, I immediately leap again, in a spectacular monster-avoiding way, and quickly check the cake. Oh Lordy Lordy, the cake has been eaten!

Not only that, there's a small silver key sitting right where the cake was.

Now I'm absolutely sure monsters don't have keys, because they live in lakes or forests or caves, and none of these places have doors that need to be locked.

So who ate the cake under my bed?

And what is the key for?

I'll have to ring Olive Higgie, code name O.H., second-in-charge and sharer-of-all-mysteries.

'O.H.,' I say. 'What hides under a bed, eats chocolate ripple cake and owns a small silver key?'

O.H. says,
'That's a hard question.
Do you have an easier one?'

I say,
'Not right now.
This is urgent.
There's something
under my bed. It
could be dangerous.'

O.H. says,
'We should feed it some pickles.'

'I don't think so. I think we need to set a trap.
A very clever, tricky kind of a trap.
I have a feeling this is a clever,
tricky kind of creature.'

O.H. says,
'Exactly! That's why pickles should
be part of the trap because
only very clever and tricky
kinds of creatures like them.'

I'm not so sure, but I don't want a disagreement. Some things are worth causing a bit of bother about, like chocolate ripple cake, or true love and bruises, but not pickles.

So after a lot of thinking and thinking, and a bit of laughing and jumping and creeping and acting like monsters, this is what we come up with:

'What will you do, once it's trapped?' says O.H. 'I mean, what if it has sharp gnashing teeth and a long thrashing tail and huge grasping claws? And what if it's very, very angry at you for trapping it with a pickle?'

'Well, if that's the case,' I say, 'I'll just have to draw on my extraterrestrial courage and intelligence, as always.' But of course what I really plan to do is run and jump on Mum and Dad's bed, and yell HELP all the way there.

Night-time

When Mum tucks me into bed, she says, 'Henrietta, tell me, why is there a pickle on a plate on the floor?'

'It's a trap to catch the creature under my bed.'

'What an excellent idea,' she says.

And then she laughs, and so I laugh. It's splendid to laugh, but it's tiring to feel splendid, so I drift off to sleep and dream that Uncle George is eating pickles with a rhino and I'm hiding behind a palm tree just in case the rhino is in a mood for charging. So I'm being quiet, quiet, quiet, when…

TING A LING A LING A LING

The bell rings right in my ear. I almost jump out of the bed in fright and sheezamageeza you won't believe what I see.

It's not a monster or a crocodile or a rhino or an elephant. It's a very tiny person with wings. And she's laughing.

'It's rude to laugh,' I say.

'Oops, is it? I thought it was very good to laugh,' she says.

'Hmmmph,' I say.

'Well, most of the time it *is* good to laugh, but not when someone nearly has a heart attack because a bell has been rung in their ear.'

'Well,' she says, putting her hands on her hips. 'It's also rude to try to trap a fairy with pickles when everyone knows chocolate is much nicer than pickles.'

'Lordy Lordy,' I say. 'Are you a fairy?'

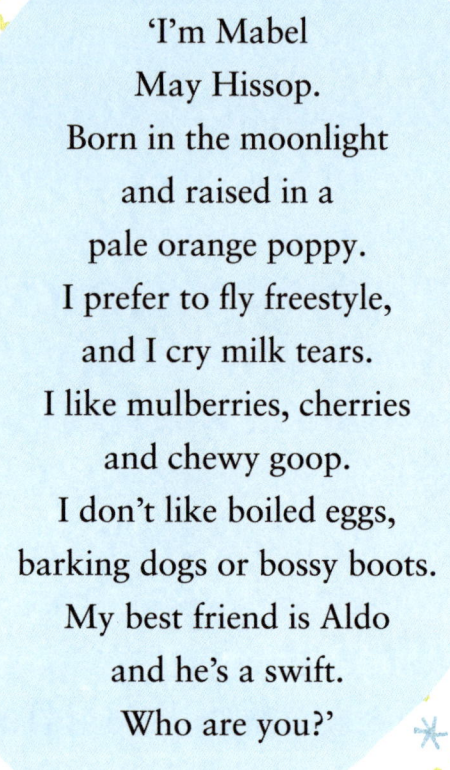

'I'm Mabel
May Hissop.
Born in the moonlight
and raised in a
pale orange poppy.
I prefer to fly freestyle,
and I cry milk tears.
I like mulberries, cherries
and chewy goop.
I don't like boiled eggs,
barking dogs or bossy boots.
My best friend is Aldo
and he's a swift.
Who are you?'

'I'm Henrietta the great go-getter.
I like chocolate ripple cake and cuddles.
I don't like pickles or whingers,
and I plan to be Queen one day.
I've been to the Wide Wide
Long Cool Coast of the Lost Socks.
Have you?'

'No, but I've visited the
Great Golden Palace
of the Queen Bee, and journeyed
on a breeze. Have you done that?'

'No, but I've climbed an apple tree
and waited in the leaves.'

'What did you wait for?'

'For nothing. I just sat
there because it was nice
next to the leaves.'

'Very good. I'm impressed,'
says Mabel. 'I knew I chose
the right sock to sleep in.'

'Have you been sleeping in my sock?'

Mabel darts under the bed, drags out my
red striped sock and wriggles inside.

'Yes, and I'm very tired now, so go back to bed
and I'll tell you the plan in the morning.'

'Plan? What plan?' I say,
but Mabel seems to
have fallen asleep.

To tell you the truth, I'm not used to fairies sleeping in my sock and I prefer to make up my own plans. In fact, I'm a great maker-upperer of plans and a great asker-of-questions. I have a whole head full of questions for Mabel. While I'm thinking, Mabel calls out, 'Oody oody, please stop thinking so loudly. If you have questions, write them down and I'll answer them in the morning.'

So I quickly write my questions and then, even though I intend to stay awake all night just to keep an eye on Mabel May Hissop, I fall instantly asleep.

When I wake up, the sun is already beaming in the window. Mabel is still fast asleep in my sock and a little breeze puffs my list of questions right onto my lap.

Magic, I think to myself. There's magic in the air. There must be, because now all the questions have been answered.

Henrietta's list of questions

Where do fairies sleep?

Wherever they want to. Under oak leaves, in tree hollows, on clouds, in hammocks hanging from stars. I have a friend who sleeps on a spider web. I prefer to be under flowerpots on a bed of rose petals. But certain types of fairies like to sleep up high, in abandoned bird nests or chimney pots or peg baskets on washing lines.

What do fairies do during the day?

Sing songs, fly around, dance, smell flowers, do somersaults, make friends, chatter and snooze.

Can you make wishes come true?

Yes, sometimes. You have to practise. Once I turned Aldo into a worm by mistake. He was very grumpy about that.

do you have a mother or a father or a brother or a sister?

No, all fairies belong to the same family. There are no parents and no children. If a fairy needs advice there are wizards and other wise creatures who can tell you useful things.

are there boy fairies?

No, there are elves who are boys.

can you talk to dogs or horses or worms?

Worms don't speak. I can talk dog and horse and bird and cat and cow, though cows don't usually have much to say.

do you whinge?

Never. Whingeing is bad for your voice and all fairies like to sing.

who is the boss of all fairies?

Me. Not Really. Everyone only bosses themselves. It's against fairy law to boss anyone but yourself.

do you get cross?

Getting cross makes your heart feeble. But everyone gets cross sometimes, even wizards and worms. Fairies try to get their crossness out of their hearts quickly, and then they sing a song or do a dance to put the good feelings back in their heart again.

what's the silver key for?

I'm not telling yet.

do fairies fall in love and get married?

Fairies are very good at falling in love but not very good at getting married.

is there anything else I should know?

My favourite colour is green. I am most well known for inventing the flying freestyle loop. My favourite dance is the lady bug boogie. It's impossible to trap a fairy but very good luck to have one under your bed. The best way to wake up a fairy is to tickle her toes with a feather while singing a dreamy kind of song.

⋆ ⋆ ⋆ ⋆

Hmm, I think to myself, how do you tickle the toes of a fairy when the fairy is inside a sock? Exactly as I am pondering this, more writing appears on the paper:

If a fairy is sleeping in a sock and her toes aren't available for tickling, then tickle her cheeks instead.

Luckily I happen to have a collection of feathers in a box. But when I tickle Mabel's cheek, she opens one eye and not the other.

She whispers, 'Please sing. It's terrible to be woken up without singing.' And then she closes her eye and goes back to sleep.

I sing Uncle George's favourite song. 'You are my sunshine, my only sunshine. You make me happy when pies are gay…'

Suddenly Mabel's wings begin to twitch and then she wriggles out, wide awake.

'That's better,' she says. 'But when are pies gay?' Before I can find an answer she says, 'Always, I suppose, especially if they are made of mulberries.' Then she starts springing up and down, up and down like a yoyo, puffing. 'Excuse my jumping, it's my morning exercises.'

Now that it's light, I can see Mabel better. If you stood her next to a dandelion, she'd be just as tall but not as thin. She's wearing white stockings, with a hole where her big toe pokes through.

She has a laughing, grinning, sparkling face.
It makes me grin too, and then I start jumping
up and down. So we are jumping together.

'Is this magic?' I say.

Mabel says, 'If you think so, then it is.'

'Mabel, you are the first fairy I have ever jumped
up and down with, and this is the first magic
I've ever felt.'

Mabel says, 'I'm sure you have felt magic before. You just didn't know what it was.' She floats down and sits on my corduroy donkey. 'Any more

questions?'

'Yes. Why are you sleeping in my sock under my bed?'

'Good question. I have a problem, of course, and I need someone to help me.' I feel a bit special when Mabel says this.

'So, what's your problem?' I say, just like a good doctor.

'I've fallen in love with Bendle Bristlemouth, the naughty Elf of Endgarden. But Bendle has not yet fallen in love with me.'

'Drats,' says I, sympathetically. I intend to fall in love with a boy who has good ideas and a lion-heart who loves me back. I don't know how I can help Mabel, because I'm not yet a love expert.

'You can help me,' says Mabel. Right then I realise that Mabel can hear my thoughts.

'Bendle is a very charming elf, and all the fairies fall in love with him. In fact, he's just like your Uncle George. So, the plan is for you to find out what impresses Uncle George the most. I mean, what exactly should a lady do to make him fall in love with her?'

'Mabel,' I say in a serious tone, 'you do realise that Uncle George is a scallywag, don't you?'

'Of course I do. Fairies are always fond of scallywags, because somewhere in the very distant past we are slightly, very slightly, related to the Scallywag family.'

'Mabel,' I say in a thoughtful tone, 'why don't you ask Uncle George yourself?'

'Because grown-ups can't see or hear fairies. It's only possible to see something if you believe in it. Which is why the more things you believe in, the bigger the world becomes.'

'Mabel,' I say knowingly, 'that's very true and I intend to have the biggest possible world ever.'

'And do you intend to tidy up that world?' says my mum, who has just walked in with Albert on her hip.

Obviously she can't see Mabel, because she ignores her completely and gives me a kiss and says there's porridge for breakfast, and afterwards she and I are going to tidy up my room. Albert points a grubby finger at Mabel, who is laughing and flying out the window into the wide blue air.

Drats. I'd rather fly out my window than tidy my room.

The hat plan

Here I am with O.H. in the garden.

O.H. is looking for Mabel under leaves and inside flowers, but I have a feeling Mabel will only be found if Mabel wants to be found, so I'm only half looking and half thinking.

'Here's an acorn lid. Maybe Mabel can wear it as a hat?' says O.H.

'It's funny you speak about hats, O.H., because I've been hatching a hat plan.'

'A hat plan?'

'Yes. You see, Uncle George always likes a hat and I thought we could make a hat that's tall enough to fit Mabel inside, so she can listen while we ask him about what makes him fall in love.'

'Excellent plot!' says O.H.

We're both pleased because it's a fine thing to hatch a secret plan.

Once the hat is finished
and O.H. has gone home,
I try it on Albert.
Then I try a question on Dad,
since Mum is at a yoga class.
'Dad, why do you love Mum?'
Dad, who's chopping
cabbage for soup, says,
'Well, I love your mum
because I just do.
Just like you love her.'
I say, 'No no. I mean why did you fall in love
with Mum and not the other ladies?'
Dad laughs, 'Well, because she was lovely. And
because she was a good dancer and a terrible cook.
And also I liked the confused look
in her eyes when she tried to sew.'
'Hmmmmm,' I say.
I'm not sure if this will be
helpful information
for Mabel or not.

Night-time again

Before I go to bed, I write a note.

> dear Mabel
> please come back.
> I have a plan.
>   love Henrietta

I fold it up in this shape

and then I throw it out into the night.

'What are you throwing that out there for?' says Mabel.

'Mabel, I wish you wouldn't just appear and disappear like that. It's very hard to make plans for someone who is unpredictable.'

'But I'm busy preparing for the annual Big Bunch of Small Creatures Ball. Bendle Bristlemouth will be there, of course, so I'm practising my moves and collecting my potions.'

'Well, I gather you already know my plan for Uncle George, so I'm not going to tell you.'

I say it a little bit huffily, because it's quite annoying dealing with a fairy who knows your secret thoughts and has read your secret letter even before you've sent it out into the sky.

The great thing about O.H. is that we talk about things and work things out together. Whereas Mabel seems to know everything already.

Mabel must be listening to my thoughts again, because she floats over and lands on my shoulder. Then she kisses me on the cheek and says, 'Thank you for helping me. I'm very grateful. And if you don't want me to listen to your thoughts, just put your hands over your ears. Then I won't be able to hear them.'
She jumps down, folds her wings in and wriggles into the sock.

I hop into bed and put my hands over my ears. But I forget to keep them there because just as I wonder what the

Big Bunch of Small Creatures Ball is,

a small silver envelope flies in the window. Inside there's an invitation.

Henrietta P. Hoppenbeek is invited to the

Big Bunch of Small Creatures Ball

WHERE: The doorway on Thistle Lane
WHEN: November Full Moon
TIME: The Quiet Hour

Suddenly I feel very excited. Imagine me, Henrietta P. Hoppenbeek the First, at the

Big Bunch of Small Creatures Ball

I'm squirming and wriggling in bed because
the idea of it is just too squirmingly good,
when Mabel calls up from her sock.
'And in case you're wondering,
the key is for the doorway on Thistle Lane.
Now please stop wriggling and go to sleep.
Otherwise you'll be too tired for the ball.'

Uncle George and I are out walking,
as that is what Uncle George likes to do
when he's wearing a new hat.
Mabel is very well installed inside it.
There's a little ledge for her to sit on
and two holes so that she can see out.
Unfortunately, Olive Higgie is at the dentist,
which is a terrible place to be,
and I'm feeling very sorry for her.

'Uncle George,' I say. 'What kind of a lady do you like to fall in love with?'

large ones   small ones   loud ones

'Well, you know me. My problem is I fall in love with all the ladies – big ones, small ones, loud ones, quiet ones, fancy ones, plain ones, messy ones, neat ones, serious ones, funny ones, relaxed ones, bossy ones and…Well, actually, that's not quite true. I'm not keen on the bossy ones.'

quiet ones   fancy ones   plain ones

Mabel whispers, 'Can you ask him to be more specific, please?'

So I say, 'Uncle George, just say that I had fallen in love with someone and I wanted that someone to ask me to a dance. What should I do to make him ask me?'

Uncle George tips the hat and whistles,
and Mabel nearly falls out.
Then he says,
in a very serious
grown-up tone,
'Well, Henrietta,
the best thing to do
is to be yourself.
After many long years
in the business of love,
I have discovered
that the most lovable lady
is one who is not afraid
to be true to herself.
It's not so easy.
People are always trying
to impress each other.
But I always *always*
fall in love with someone
who isn't trying too hard
to impress me.

That's why I'm now in love
with Miss Lily Fantuzzi.
However,
a fetching dress is always helpful.'
'But how do you be yourself?'
'Well, you say what you really think
instead of what you think someone
might want you to say.
You dance in your own way,
without worrying how it looks.
You wear your favourite dress,
not the one you think
other people will like.
And you laugh at things
you find funny,
and you don't laugh
if something is not funny,
and…'
'Okay, okay I get it.'

Uncle George has a sunny look on his face, as if he's feeling all smoochy just thinking about love. Then he stops suddenly and says, 'How odd, I just felt the hat lift off my head.'

Mabel flies off with a sparkling grin on her face, doing big loops in the sky as she goes.

I wonder if Uncle George almost believes in something, because it looks as if he's watching her go.

Then he laughs and picks me up and puts me on his shoulders. 'Anyway, Henrietta, you're already an absolute being-yourself-expert, so all I'd say to you is don't go changing for anyone.'

The Big Bunch of Small Creatures Ball

It's midnight and Mabel and I are off to the ball.
Mabel is wearing her favourite dress,
which is green, of course, with spots.
I'm wearing my favourite dress,
which is red, of course, with yellow flowers.
I'm also wearing Uncle George's hat,
because he forgot to take it home
and I think the hat deserves
to come to the ball.
Mabel has a crown of dandelions.

'Mabel, will I be too big for the ball?'

'You'll be the biggest creature there. Isn't that something?'

'I guess so. Who else will be there?'

'Oody oody, wait and see.'
Mabel sits on my shoulder
and flutters her wings.

The doorway on Thistle Lane is not at all like the entrance to a ball. Long weeds scrounge around the bottom, and a web of ivy wriggles up the face of it. But then I notice that the keyhole is glowing and pulsing with silver light.

It makes me feel all fizzy inside, and I can tell
Mabel is feeling all fluttery too,
because her wings don't stop moving.
I put the silver key in the lock and slowly,
slowly push open the door.

Lordy Lordy, what a sight.

It's a big room with crumbly old stone walls and no roof. The sky is all lit up with stars and swishes of moving lights.

'They're fireflies,' whispers Mabel.

There are fairies everywhere, darting and hovering.

And elves dancing and stomping and singing, holding hands and flinging their legs up and weaving through the crowd in big circles. In the middle, a group of small folk play fiddles and bells. A fat little elf with a white beard and a curly green hat hoots as he bangs a tyre with a drumstick.

The music is fast and loud and it almost feels like a wave that might take you up and whirl you around.

'Dance, then, if you want to,' sings Mabel. 'Come on.' She floats off into the air and does a beautiful swirl.

I watch the butterflies and dragonflies and ladybirds buzzing about in the air. Everyone is so delicate and small that I feel a bit shy, for once in my life. I take off my hat and squish myself down to be as small as possible, which is quite uncomfortable.

Just as I am watching two ladybirds playing leap-frog with a dragonfly, a fairy falls from the sky and lands on her bottom right in front of me. I jump up to see if she is all right but, before I even take a step, a bird lands on my shoulder and whispers, 'Never help a fairy who's fallen from the sky. It only hurts their pride to fall. It doesn't hurt their bottoms.'

'Oh,' I say, as if it's perfectly normal to have a bird telling you what to do, though actually I feel strange and giddy and excited.

'I'm Aldo, Mabel's best friend. Henrietta, I presume?' says the bird.

'That's right. Henrietta the great go-getter.'

'The great go-getter indeed. Well, shall we go get a good time then? Mabel has charged me to look after you while she's engaged in Bendle Bristlemouth's tedious shenanigans.'

Aldo sighs and points his wing to the corner of the room.

A circle of fairies sit at the feet of a red-cheeked elf, who is busy laughing and gesturing and pointing all at once.

Mabel is gazing up at him.

'What are they doing?' I ask Aldo, since I'm not sure what 'tedious shenanigans' are.

'Oh, the little love-struck twits just sit there while Bendle thinks up naughty pranks and then watches as they do his mischief for him. Look at that fairy dangling a silk thread over the nose of that poor old elf.

Aldo swoops over and plucks the silk thread
out of the fairy's hand, as the old elf
is sniffing and sneezing.
'Aldo,' I say seriously. 'Surely
Mabel isn't a twit?'
'Mabel is usually a very smart fairy,
but love does strange things to us all.
It looks like she is next in line, too.
Oh, dear me. Shall we dance, Henrietta?'
'Oh no, I can't dance here.
I'm too big. I'd be embarrassed.
And anyway, shouldn't we
help Mabel?'
'Remember the rule
of the fallen fairy.
You can't help a fairy.
Not unless she asks you to.'

Mabel did ask me to help. But I don't really feel like helping her to win over Bendle Bristlemouth, I feel like helping her to lose him. But if that's not technically allowed, then what can I do?

'Dance!' says a voice from below my knees. It's a ragged little elf whose curly hair seems to be shining, or is it his eyes shining? He winks and then runs off, doing cartwheels, leaping and throwing his arms around wildly. I make myself small again and try to dance just like a fairy, delicately, in the manner of a flower, but it isn't any fun at all. The shining-eyed elf is laughing and I think of Uncle George, with the shine in his eyes.

Suddenly I know how to help Mabel.

I dance the Henrietta P. Hoppenbeek Dance, wild and wide, spinning and leaping. And I don't care that I'm different from everyone else here. I dance just how I want to dance.

I see bats swooping and silkworms glowing and birds darting and dark misty lake bugs scuttling, and then I see Mabel hovering right in front of my nose, frowning.

She says, 'Henrietta, oh dear, Bendle has told me to trip you up and make a fool of you.'

'But there's no need, Mabel. I'm making a fool of myself and it's great fun.'

Mabel stops very still in the air and looks at me in a perplexed way. Slowly she starts grinning, and then laughing.

She whispers to me, 'Henrietta, isn't it something to be the biggest creature here?'

She whirls her wonderful circles as I wave my wild laughing arms and together we are dancing and looping and leaping for joy. And then Aldo joins us, and so does the elf with the shining eyes. Soon there's a whole circle of creatures whirling around me.

Soon it's just Mabel and me and Aldo and the shining-eyed elf – whose name is Melo – sitting in a circle on the grass. We have been talking and drinking mulberry juice out of gumnut cups. Around us the party is beginning to quieten down, the music is slow and some creatures are leaving.

I notice that Mabel and Melo are holding hands and smiling at each other, just like Uncle George does when he's in love.

'Aldo,' I say dreamily. 'I think it's time for me to go home now. Would you show me the way?'

'I'd be delighted,' says Aldo.

We wave goodbye to Mabel and Melo, and as we wander home I ask Aldo if he thinks they are in love.

'Who knows?'

'Yes, who knows?' I say philosophically, because I would never have known that the last piece of chocolate ripple cake could lead to a Big Bunch of Small Creatures Ball. And now I do.

Waking up

Next morning, I hear Albert talking to himself, in Albert language. Dad is singing in the shower, 'You are my sunshine, my only sunshine, you make me happy when pies are gay.' I leap out of bed and look in the sock, but Mabel isn't there.

Albert is happy to see me though, and I do particularly care about Albert after all. He stands up in his cot and says, 'Al awake now.'

'Albert, there's something I have to tell you about growing up.'

Albert repeats, 'Al awake now.'

'Albert, listen. This is important information. Be very careful not to become one of those grown-ups who think that certain things aren't really real, like sea monsters and Martians, and stars that guide you, and wishes that come true, and lands ruled by lost socks, and creatures that need to laugh. And also, it's much better to give the last piece of cake to someone else than to eat it yourself.'

Albert bangs the cot with his hand and says, 'Up now.' So I gather he's got the message.

Anyway, just talking about stars and wishes and creatures makes me feel all excited about the day and all the discoveries I might make.

I throw on my most splendid dress, and just as I'm about to hoon out the door to tell O.H. all about the ball, another envelope comes zigzagging in the window.

> Dear Henrietta,
> Thank you for letting me sleep in your sock.
> Thank you especially for helping me lose
> Bendle Bristlemouth
> and find Melo Merrytoe.
> I am very pleased to know you.
> Aldo thinks you are the very very finest
> dancing partner. I do too.
> Bye bye, or as we fairies say, eye bye
> (which means: look out for me, I'll be nearby).
> Love Mabel
> P.S. Melo and I are eating honey
> on the wild white plains of Peasebury.

I'm not sure, but maybe I also hear a little giggle and some humming wings, but it might just be my imagination. Dad says I have a very healthy one.

HENRIETTA
and the Perfect Night

Back where it all began...

To the possum.

The Waiting Game

Hello, I'm Henrietta the Great Go-Getter. I'm an only child. I'm also a Big Thinker. And right now I'm thinking about my mum getting fat. This sometimes happens to mums and dads. Dads also lose the hair on their head. Poor dads. I wouldn't like to lose my hair because it's good for making up hairstyles. Like this.

All kinds of things change with mums and dads. Hair goes grey. Noses get bigger. Wrinkles and crinkles appear. But inside they're still your mum and dad who love you. And I don't mind one bit if they change on the outside.

My mum isn't really getting fat. It's just that there's a baby growing inside her and one day it will come out.

'What sort of baby?' I ask.

'We don't know yet.'

'Will it be a nice one?'

'All babies are nice.'

'A little sister?'

'Maybe, or a little brother. We'll have to wait and see.'

I'm terrible at waiting.

Mum says I must learn to be patient. But I say there are more exciting things to learn than patience. Like how to fly to the moon. How to tap dance. How to cook pavlova. Patience is for flowers in the field, and teachers of little kids, and for mums.

What's more, I already know I want a baby sister, not a baby brother. What can you do with brothers? Boys are bossy and noisy. But a little sister – she'll smell just right, like roses and sweets and streams and kittens. She'll love tap dancing, and I'll carry her everywhere and dress her up in different sorts of hats, and one day I'll teach her how to catch bugs, and how to play snap. I may even let her win. Sometimes.

'How much longer do I have to wait for my baby sister?' I say.

'Six more months,' says Dad.

'How long is six months?'

'Halfway to Christmas.'

'That's a lot of waiting!'

'That's because the baby needs to be properly cooked.'

'Dad, it's not a cake, it's a baby.'

Sometimes my dad forgets what's what. Lucky I'm here to put him straight.

'You're right, it isn't a cake. But, speaking of cakes, since we have to wait six months for a baby and only half an hour for a cake, how about we bake a chocolate ripple cake right now?'

Who says no to cake? Not me. But I've had chocolate ripple cake before and it didn't make me patient. I'm not convinced it will make me patient now. Cake or no cake, I have discoveries to make.

'But, Dad, why does it take so long to grow a baby?'

'Because at first a baby is as small as a seed in the ground, only it's a seed inside a mum. And you know how long it takes for a seed to grow.'

I have a think about this.

I already happen to know that seeds are slow, and they need sun and water and loving care, because we planted sunflowers and I had to dribble the hose on them carefully whenever it was hot. But you can't water a seed inside your mum's tummy, or show it the sun.

'But what makes the seed inside Mum grow?' I ask my dad.

Dad has a think about this. My dad's a big thinker, like me.

'Daddy's love started it going, and Mum's body keeps it growing,' he says. Then he takes me outside.

'See the apple tree? Once, that tree was just a seed in the ground, and now it's big enough to grow apples. By the end of summer those apples will be big enough for apple crumble. Do you know what season it will be when we eat apple crumble?'

'Autumn!' I say.

'Yes, autumn, when the leaves change colour and drop off. Then comes winter, when there's no fruit or leaves, just the cold, bare branches. But once little buds start growing again, then you'll know it's time for the baby to come.'

'In spring?'

'Yes, in spring.'

So, when buds show on the apple tree, my waiting will be over. Finally.

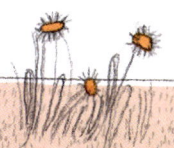

Still, that's a very long time,

still I have no patience.

The very next day I check the apples to see if they've grown bigger, but they haven't. I'm worried. This will take a very long time if they don't start growing soon. Maybe they forgot to grow. Or maybe they need loving care.

I could kiss them, but it would be too hard to kiss the ones up high, and you can't really have favourites. That wouldn't be fair.

And there are so many apples to give presents to, and so many to whisper kind words to. I have an idea. I'll sing them a lullaby. That's how Mum gets me to sleep. I go and find Mum's ukulele, then I climb up the tree.

Only I don't know how to play the ukulele. It's harder than I thought, but surely not too hard. I climb down again and run inside. Dad is baking his cake and Mum has put her feet up.

I say, 'Can you show me how to play a song for the apples?'

'Why do you want to play a song for the apples?' says Mum.

'Because I want to give them some loving care, so they grow faster, so the tree loses its leaves faster, and then it will soon be time for the baby to come.'

'Good idea,' says Mum.

So we go outside and sit under the tree together, and Mum tries to teach me to play the ukulele. But after a while I say she can play and I'll sing, as I have no patience for learning to play the ukulele but I do have a mouth to sing with.

Everyone does. (Except worms. Poor worms. They can't sing. And maybe fish can't sing, either, since they're underwater.)

'Sing loud,' says Mum, 'because the baby will hear you, and maybe it will grow faster so it can meet you.'

I've never thought about the baby meeting me. Will my baby sister like me? Will she be pleased that I, Henrietta the Great Go-Getter, am her big sister? Sometimes I can be bossy. And I've never been a big sister. I need to practise. One thing about me is I have great-go-get-it determination.

'Enough singing now,' I say. I don't want to hurry my baby sister, after all. First I need to practise being a big sister.

I squeeze through the hole in my fence and skip down the street to Eloise's house. Eloise is only two years old. I can practise being a big sister with Eloise.

Eloise is in her garden, in the sand pit. She's filling cups with sand and pouring the sand out again. I sit in the sand with Eloise. She's happy to see me. Little girls always like big girls.

I say, 'How about we build a sandcastle together?'

Eloise is excited about my idea. Already I'm being a good pretend big sister. But Eloise stomps on my sandcastle. She thinks this is very funny. Obviously, you can't expect little sisters to respect sandcastles. I've already learnt something.

After that, Eloise wants to play Ring a Ring a Rosie. She especially likes the bit when we both fall down. She says, 'Again?' So we do it again.

And again. And again. Until finally I say, 'No more.' Enough is enough. There are only so many times you can play.

But then Eloise starts to cry. In fact she begins to wail and stomp, and soon she's screaming and getting red in the face. She turns into a terrible monster, right before my eyes. It's like magic. Sheezamageeza! Am I in big trouble?

Her mum comes and picks her up, but she isn't cross. She says, 'Eloise is very tired, that's all.'

Well, as a matter of fact, I'm very extremely tired, too, but it doesn't turn me into a monster. I am still me. It's hard work practising to be a big sister. I trudge home. It looks like I'm not quite ready for a baby sister.

But at least I've learnt some patience. Now I know I can wait halfway to Christmas. The apples can grow as slowly as they like. I can wait for the buds in spring. Patience isn't as hard as I thought.

When I walk in our door, I smell chocolate ripple cake. And it's ready right now! No waiting necessary.

The First Day

If you're wondering why I'm known as
Henrietta the Great Go-Getter,
it's because of my adventurous spirit and
my **great** determination. I'm an explorer
of life, and that includes trees, bugs, animals
and all mysteries.

But, I should warn you, the truth is `I'm really very shy.` If you met me you would see. Here's a secret. Shy people pretend they're great adventurers so that no one knows how shy they really are.

I'm going to school. For the very first time.
My first day.

I have a new lunch box with a cheese sandwich in it. I wanted peanut butter, but peanut butter is dangerous for allergic kids so you can't have it at school.

Imagine being slayed by a peanut!
Better to **fight a dragon** or get captured
by a flying saucer.

Last night I shined my shoes with Mum's hairspray. Mum said hairspray is for making shiny hair, not shiny shoes. Oh well. Now I know. Mum showed me the shoe polish in a round tin.

It smelled worse than hairspray but it worked better. I like the way my shoes look ready for school. And I like the way I have a new pack with my lunch box ready inside. I am ready all over.

Or am I?

Now that all the preparing is done, I'm suddenly not so sure. After all, I have a nice house here with doors to slam, and a biscuit tin on the top shelf, and a hole in the fence for sneaking through, and a garden with an apple tree.

What more does a kid need?

'Mum, I don't want to go to school today. I'd rather stay home and play games with you.'

Mum says, 'But Henrietta, I know you'll really like school once you're used to it.'

And I say, 'No, actually, I think I already like the way things are here. So I might just go and hide in the cupboard now.'

While I'm hiding in the cupboard, waiting for Mum to find me, I try to imagine what school will be like. Will I have to sit still all day long? Will I get into trouble if I wriggle even a little bit? Will there be bullies and mean kids?

I hear a knock on the cupboard door. Mum has found me.

'Are you in there?'
'No.'

Mum says, 'Well that's a shame because I've thought up a game that Henrietta would love to play, if only I could find her.'

I pop my head out. 'Look! Surprise, surprise. Here I am after all.'

Mum whispers, 'How about we play spies? We can walk to school and just have a secret peep inside.'

Mum sometimes does have excellent ideas. Spying on school. Imagine.

'But I'll be the head spy?'

'Yes,' says Mum.

'And then we come home again?'

'Yes,' says Mum. 'Then we come home.'

On the way we see a spider web with a bee stuck in it. Since I'm the head spy, I hatch a plan to free the bee at once. Spies are obliged to perform rescues whenever they can. Especially if it's to rescue a honey-making creature.

So we *unstick the bee* and watch it fly away. It forgets to say thank you. That's how it is in nature.

Then we meet the lollipop lady. She wears a yellow coat and holds a sign like this:

Her name is Beverly. She makes us stand behind the line until she blows her whistle. She's like a sergeant major.

Mum whispers to me, 'At school there are rules.'

Obviously, we need to practise standing behind the line like real school children. We pretend to be obedient, but really we're secret spies trying to uncover secrets.

So I have to poke my shiny shoe a tiny bit over the line, just to see what Beverly will do. Will she explode?

But she's too busy telling other kids to stand behind the line. You can see she likes the sergeant major job.

When we get to school there's a hook with my name on it, outside the classroom.

I do like a hook that's ready and waiting just for me. But it doesn't say 'Henrietta the Great Go-Getter', it only says 'Henrietta Hopkins'. Since we're just spying, I won't correct the hook. Not yet.

We peek around the door. There is not one single kid I know.

How can I play with kids I don't know? Even spies feel shy. What a conundrum, which, if you don't know,
is a tangled-up situation that can't quite be untangled. My mum sneaks us inside the classroom.

We're undercover. I stand next to Mum and pretend I'm busy. I count the crayons in a box. Spies always count things. I think of my apple tree at home. I think about the teacher with her black curly hair and round glasses. Will she make me eat zucchini, or check I brushed my teeth, or tell me my hair is in knots?

She says, 'Hello. Who have we got here?'

I say, 'I'm not staying at school. We're just looking, thank you.'

My mum says, 'This is Henrietta.'

The teacher says, 'Henrietta, maybe you'd like to stay for a little while?'

'No thank you. I'm going home very soon. We have some rescues to do,' says I.

Just then someone starts to cry. It's a girl with plaits. She's wearing denim shorts and carrying a wombat. She doesn't want to stay at school, either, but her mum has left her here. I wouldn't like that. I hold my mum's hand, just to make sure.

The teacher tries to comfort the girl. If I was that girl I wouldn't feel comforted by a grown-up I'd never ever met before, even if she was the kindest person in the world.

I have a good idea.

I will comfort the crying girl because I'm new, just like her, and I know exactly how she feels. And I know how to perform rescues because I'm a secret spy who has already rescued a bee.

I let go of Mum's hand, walk up close and say, 'Hello.'

The girl looks at me. She's still crying, so she can't say hello back, but I understand. So I say, 'Would you like to come and see the crayons with me?'

She nods.

I hold her hand and take her over to the crayon box. 'Let's write our names on pieces of paper,' I say.

She stops crying now. She looks astonished. She says, 'But I can't write yet.'

And I say, 'That's not one bit of a problem because I can't either, so let's draw our houses instead.'

We start drawing our houses.

Soon the crying girl is having a nice time. She even asks me a question.

'What's your name?'

'Henrietta Hopkins,' I say, so as not to frighten her with my title. 'What's yours?'
'Olive Higgie.'
'That rhymes with piggy,' I say. And then I chuckle. And luckily Olive Higgie chuckles too. It's important to have a sense of humour when you're at school for the first time.

My mum says, 'Do you want to come home now, Henrietta?' And I whisper to her that I'm afraid I'll have to stay at school and look after Olive Higgie, as it's her first day and she's very shy and doesn't know anyone else except ME. Spies have to look after frightened people. It's a rescue mission.

Mum agrees that this is an important job. And after she leaves, Olive Higgie and I start to draw pigs on the piece of paper. Like this:

We draw all kinds of animals, even made-up ones. Like this:

We're having such a good time we almost forget it's our first day of school and we're very shy and there are rules.

The teacher says, 'It's time to begin. Come and sit in a circle.' Our first rule.

Olive Higgie and I sit next to each other. Let me share another secret.

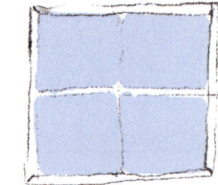

You only need one friend in a room
full of strangers to feel perfectly happy.
To tell the truth, since truth is something
I like to tell, I don't know if I rescued
Olive Higgie, or if she rescued me, or if
we rescued each other, but now perhaps
I will like school after all.

the Sleepover

Sheezamageeza. You'll never guess.

I'm invited to my friend Olive Higgie's house for a sleepover. Me, Henrietta the Great Go-Getter. I have never ever in my life been for a sleepover.

But don't worry, I'm not one bit nervous. I'm extremely excited. And I have a sleeping bag with leopard skin on the inside. Just hear me roar.

I pack all the things I'll need. My spotty pyjamas, of course. Mr Nelson, who is my knitted monkey, only for in bed at night. My toothbrush for keeping the dentist away, and my hairbrush because Olive Higgie does like to play hairdressers.

My `secret diary` because I may want to write something secret at any moment. My `gumboots` in case we go out stomping in the rain. And my `sleeping bag`, of course. My `hula hoop` in case I want to put on a circus. But the hula hoop won't actually fit in the bag.

Never mind, I'll just carry it along anyway.

Mum says, 'What about clean clothes for tomorrow?'

Tomorrow? I always forget to think about tomorrow. Hula hoops are more important than tomorrow.

Olive Higgie's house is green. There's a ginger cat in the front garden. Olive Higgie comes to the door. She's just as excited as I am. She has made apricot slice for afternoon tea, and even set the table with lavender in the middle. We sit at the table, eating apricot slice for afternoon tea, like two ladies.

I wave goodbye to Mum. I'm not one bit sad to see her leave. I feel quite grown-up now that I'm having my first sleepover.

Olive Higgie has an older brother called Max. He does disgusting things like pulling apart dead cockroaches in front of us when we're trying to eat apricot slice. He also likes to throw things (cockroaches, rotten plums, water bombs) at us. Or wrestle.
Or spy on us. But we always catch him.

'Max. We can see you're spying on us,' calls Olive Higgie.

Then she whispers to me, 'Let's do something `very, very secret`, and we won't let Max see.'

This is a fine plan. But what?

It will soon be bedtime, so we decide to hide Max's pyjamas. But where?

'Let's hang them in a tree, like a scarecrow,' I say.

Olive Higgie giggles into her hand.

This is an equally fine idea. We sneak into Max's bedroom on tip toes.

Olive Higgie slips her hand under his pillow and pulls out his pyjamas. They're blue and stripy and all crinkled up like a piece of paper. She passes me the legs half, and we stick them under our tops and sneak out like fat secret agents.

But how to hang them in the tree?

Olive Higgie says, 'Pegs will do it.'

So we peg Max's pyjamas in the tree, just like a scarecrow. The birds all fly away fast. They must think there's a pyjama monster in their tree. Poor birds.

'What if the birds want to come home to

their nests at bedtime, but they're frightened of the pyjama monster?' I ask.

Olive Higgie considers this. I do like to think of a problem and then see if Olive Higgie can figure it out. She's pretty good at figuring.

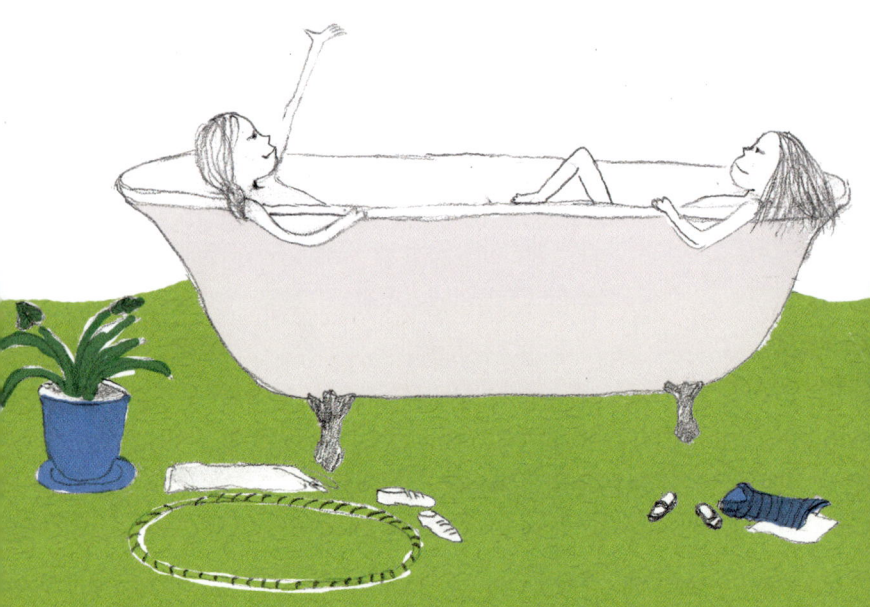

'Well,' she says, 'we'll take down the pyjama monster before it gets dark, but leave it there until Max thinks his pyjamas have run away.'

'Ha, ha, runaway pyjamas,' says I.

'He, he, stinky pyjama monster,' Olive says.

We have a good laugh and then we make up a silly hula hoop dance, which we perform for all the birds who have flown off to trees without pyjama monsters in them.

They don't say thank you, but that's how it is in nature.

All that hula hooping makes us hot and tired. We change into our bathers and pretend the bathtub is a cool swimming pool. We lie on our backs and let our hair spread out under the water like mermaids.

Olive Higgie says, 'I wouldn't really like to be a mermaid, because I wouldn't want a fish's tail. I do like running around and jumping on the trampoline.'

'Yes,' I agree. 'And breathing air and sleeping in beds and stomping, skipping, skylarking…'

I'm rudely interrupted by Max, who pokes his head around the door. Then he runs out, shouting through the house, 'Ha, ha, the girls think they're mermaids,' as if it's silly to pretend to be mermaids. But we have our own opinions about that, and we don't care one bit what boys think. We only act like we do, just for fun.

'Hmmmph,' I say, haughty as possible. 'There is such a thing as privacy.'

'Big brothers are so annoying,' agrees Olive Higgie. 'But just wait till he can't find his pyjamas. Then he'll be sorry.'

And we start to laugh again. Laughing mermaids are the very best sort. Much better than weeping ones who sit on rocks and wish they could walk.

After that it's dinnertime. We're wearing our pyjamas already. We've combed our hair one hundred times. We smell like roses because we put cream all over us after the bath, like ladies. But I can also smell dinner.

What if it's brussel sprouts, or pink fish with bones, or green salad? Things I don't like. I'm a little nervous all of a sudden, because at other people's houses you're not allowed to complain. What if it's brussel sprout salad? I'll come out in spots if I have to eat that.

'Olive,' I whisper, 'what are we having for dinner?'

Olive goes on a mission of discovery. 'Lentil soup. Do you like it?'

'Well, it's much better than brussel sprouts.' I don't say I would have preferred peanut butter sandwiches, because that would be rude.

At dinner, I watch Max to see if he suspects his pyjamas have been stolen. But Max is busy boasting about the Magpies, which is his football team. My dad barracks for the Tigers. I just barrack for me and the small creatures, which I do like to rescue whenever I can. It's important to stand up for small things. My mum says it's also important to eat vegetables, and to be kind. I eat nearly all my lentil soup, and I don't tell Max that his football team is a dud, because I'm trying to be kind.

And guess what we have for dessert?
Apple crumble! I'm particularly fond of apple crumble.

Finally it's bedtime. Finally Max is told to put his pyjamas on. Olive Higgie and I keep the straightest of faces. We wait. We keep waiting. Max comes out. He's wearing different pyjamas. Red ones with racing cars.

I look at Olive Higgie and Olive Higgie looks at me. We're very disappointed. Max doesn't even realise his other pyjamas have run away.

'What are you staring at?' he says to Olive.

'Nothing,' she says.

'Yes, nothing,' I add.

Max puts Olive in a headlock and I try to pull him off and we end up in a big fight on the carpet, which is quite good fun.

But once we're in bed, we debrief.

'The problem is boys don't notice pyjamas. Next time, we'll have to put some worms in his bed. Boys notice worms.'

Olive Higgie knows more about boys than I do.

'Would he notice if we put slime in his bed?' I ask.

'Yes,' she yawns. 'Slime and worms...'

Olive Higgie falls asleep very quick sticks. But I'm still awake. Olive Higgie's bedroom is not my bedroom, and I'm not in my bed, and usually my mum plays a song on her ukelele to help me go to sleep. I wish my mum was here, playing me a song. Maybe 'Summertime'. That's her favourite.

I look out the window. It's dark outside.
I feel all alone. Now I'm not so sure sleepovers
are a good idea. There's a whispery black tree
right near the window, full of shadowy things
and – Sheezamageeza!

I jump onto Olive Higgie's bed and wake her
up.

'There's someone in the tree! I'm scared.'

Olive Higgie sits straight up in her bed and looks out the window. Then she giggles.

'Henrietta, it's only our pyjama monster. We forgot to get it down.'

I giggle too. Then we're both giggling so much that Max comes running in and says, 'What's going on?'

Olive Higgie points out the window. 'Your pyjamas, they're standing in the tree. Look!'

And I say, 'You better get them because otherwise the birds won't fly home to their nests!'

Max looks. We can tell he isn't keen on fetching his pyjamas, but he doesn't want us to see he's scared of the dark. So he runs out there as fast as he can, pulls his pyjamas down and comes back in, white as a ghost. Then he headlocks me and Olive Higgie tries to pull me out and we all end up fighting on the carpet.

I'm tired after all that fighting, but we're very pleased we did get even with Max,
after all.

Olive Higgie sings me 'Old MacDonald had a Farm', instead of 'Summertime', even though it's the world's most boring song.
I only hear the first verse because it sends me to sleep. Instantly.

the School Play

We're doing a `school play`. All our parents are invited. We'll dress up in costumes and be proper actors and actresses. It's hard to stop thinking about it. I'm `enormously excited`, to tell the truth.

I've had a lot of practice at pretending to be someone else. That's what acting is. Sometimes I'm a dragon, breathing fire and waving my thorny tail, scaring the butterflies, and sometimes I'm singing lullabies to the apples in the apple tree. So I'll definitely be a good actress, but the problem is that Olive Higgie is even more excited than me, because when Olive Higgie grows up she's going to be a famous actress and I'm going to be an explorer.

Explorers can't be actresses as well, so I have to let Olive Higgie be more excited than me, which is hard because I'd like to be the most excited of anyone.

Our school play will be an adventure story about a man called Noah who gets all the animals on his boat before a flood comes. I would very much like to be Noah in the play, as he's the most important person in the story. He's the hero. And I also have heroic qualities, because I'm fond of a rescue.

We're sitting in a circle. The teacher has a list of who will be who in the play. I'm crossing my fingers. I don't want to be a camel, that's for sure. Camels don't make any noise. The teacher says, 'Henrietta, you will be a bat.' Then she says, 'Olive Higgie, you will be Noah.' And then she says, 'Harry Binch, you will be a camel.'

Harry Binch is very quiet, so he won't mind being a camel.

Olive Higgie is very proud and pleased to

be Noah. She claps her hands loudly. I'm a bit quiet about being the bat. I can't speak to Olive Higgie straight away, because I'm full of jealousy. It's much more special to be Noah than to be a bat. Everyone will be watching Noah. Not the bat. But at least I'm not the camel, and bats can hang upside down. Also, since Olive Higgie is my best friend, I must try to be happy for her and not sad for me. It's always much nicer to happy with someone than it is to be full of bad feelings.

So I turn to Olive Higgie and I say, 'Congratulations, Olive. You'll be the best Noah.'

And she says, 'Thank you, Henrietta. You are the only person in the class who is good at hanging upside down.'

This is true. I am a `very good upside-down-hanger`. I hang on the monkey bars. So I can feel a bit proud of being a bat, after all. And Olive and I can be pleased together, which is important when you're best friends.

The next day we start rehearsing. Olive Higgie has a lot of lines to say because Noah tells all the animals to come two by two into

the boat. But I get to say my lines while hanging upside down. Also, it doesn't take long before I add some flying and swooping moves, so the audience will be sure to see that I'm a bat. I can tell our teacher is impressed with my enthusiasm for the role, though she does keep telling me not to block off the other animals while I'm swooping.

After a while of rehearsing I realise I'm very good at being a bat, and I'm really glad I'm not Noah. I can have fun swooping and flying and hanging and beating my wings. Poor Olive Higgie must stand up straight and always be saying things.

After school Olive Higgie is quiet. Probably she's tired after all that talking. I try to cheer her up by performing some very swirly bat swoops, but this makes her even more uncheerful. Then she begins to cry, so I stop swooping. My advice is, never clown around when your friend is upset. I sit next to her and I say, 'What's wrong?'

She says, 'Well, actually, it's hard to be Noah because I'm afraid I'll never remember all the lines. And I really want to do a good job or I'll never be a famous actress.'

What a conundrum. I have a think about it.

'Olive, how about I help you learn your lines? I can pretend to be all the animals, even the camel, and you can practise saying things to me. We can do it after school or at lunch time.'

Olive Higgie opens her sad eyes wide. She smiles.

'That would be very helpful,' she says, and I can tell she feels better already.

The next day we begin our hard work, though it's much harder for Olive than for me. I enjoy pretending to be all the animals, even the camel. Some more advice I have is, if you ever have to be a camel, just chew a lot and stretch your neck long. After a while I know Olive's lines as well as Olive does, because I happen to have an excellent memory, which makes me the perfect friend to learn with. And I'm not just making that up, because Olive Higgie says to me, 'Henrietta, you are the best best friend.'

I feel much better about being a best best friend than I would have felt being Noah. What's more, my mum helps me make a really swishy bat suit. This is how I look. Very battish indeed. I do like a black cloak. Bats are really very special and mysterious and different from regular animals. Which is a bit like me.

Today's the day of the play. Our costumes are all hanging on our school hooks. I'm swooping around the classroom in anticipation. Our teacher tells me to settle down, but bats prefer to settle up. We practise the song we're going to play on our recorders.

Finally it's time to put on our costumes. Harry Binch looks perfect as a camel. He has a nice hump made of cushions. And everyone likes my bat costume. Poor Olive Higgie only gets to dress like a man, which is not so exciting, but never mind.

Then all our parents begin to arrive. We wait backstage, which is outside. Just then something terrible happens. Olive Higgie has to sit down. She's pale with fright. Stage fright. She can't even move. Our teacher looks most concerned. She says, 'Class, it looks like Olive Higgie won't be able to perform today, which means we may have to cancel our play.'

Imagine the groaning and moaning when we hear that!

Our teacher says, 'I'm sorry. This is disappointing for you, after your hard work…'

Then Olive Higgie calls out in a wobbly voice, 'Henrietta knows my lines. She could be Noah.'

Everyone looks at me. I look at everyone. For a moment my head spins. Suddenly everyone is depending on me. It will be terrible to let them down. And I do have heroic qualities, after all. Besides, I want the play to go on.

'Okay, I will be Noah,' I say.

Then there's cheering and hooting and I have to change quickly out of my swishy bat costume and into Olive's boring Noah costume. And before I even have a chance to feel shy I'm walking onto the stage and I'm saying the first words of the play: 'Welcome to the story of Noah's Ark. I am Noah …'

So the play goes on. And when it's time for the bat to appear, who should swoop in but Olive Higgie, who has recovered from her stage fright. Lucky I have an excellent memory so I don't forget any words, and lucky I've had a lot of practice being dragons

so I'm quite a natural at being Noah. And at the end of the play all the parents are clapping and clapping and I'm taking a nice big bow.

Afterwards, everyone tells me I did a very good job. My dad says he's proud of me, and my mum says it's no wonder I'm such a good Noah, because I've had a lot of practice rescuing animals from natural disasters.

And then Olive Higgie says quietly, 'You'll be a better actress than me because I get stage fright and you don't.'

But I say, 'I'd still rather be an explorer, and discover undiscovered things.'

And she says, 'Maybe I'll explore with you.'

And I say, 'Most certainly you can.'

And after that we both do some excellent bat swooping around the bare winter trees, until it's time to go home.

The Arrival

We're going on a special weekend away, to our cousin's farm, to see the baby lambs. It will be a long drive but I won't complain because I'm enormously happy about going there. Dad has cooked popcorn for the trip. We'll play all my favourite songs in the car, and watch the scenery, and look out for horses in fields. And windmills.

We'll stay the night, so I'll pack my purple backpack and take my leopard skin sleeping bag. I'd like to take my hula hoop to show my cousins how well I can hula around, but Mum says it will take up too much room in the car. Actually, it's Mum who will take up too much room, as she has a **very large stomach** with my baby sister growing inside, but I don't tell her that as you shouldn't talk about the size of anyone's stomach, especially if they're a grown-up.

Dad packs a lot of food. He has made lasagne for dinner. I LOVE lasagne and lasagne loves me. My cousins will be very happy to see me and the lasagne. The cousins are called Verity and Tom. Verity is bigger than me and Tom is littler, so that makes it fair. Verity can already ride a horse, though, and I'd really like to ride a horse too. Mum says Verity might teach me this time. Olive Higgie will be jealous of me if I ride a horse. I can't wait to tell her. I'll ask Mum to take a photo of me in action on the horse, when it's galloping over a fallen tree.

We squeeze everything into our little red car, and Mum says she hopes it won't break down as it's a very old car that does sometimes like to break down. Dad says cars only do that when you don't expect them to, so as long as we all expect our car to break down it certainly won't.

'How long do we have to keep expecting it to break down for?' I ask. I would rather think about other things, like galloping off on a horse. Dad says he thinks we've all expected it enough now. So instead we decide to sing 'Row Row Row Your Boat', in rounds.

Outside the window the world passes by. It's a nice feeling to be going somewhere. It's what I call an adventure. You can't be sure what will happen, the spirit of adventure wiggles around inside you and it begins to sing. It sings of horses and lambs and fields of flowers, as it's springtime now and flowers are peeking out everywhere.

'Who wants popcorn?' shouts Dad. He has the spirit of adventure in him too.

'Me!' says I. I throw some pieces out the window when no one is looking, just like Hansel and Gretel.

Soon we're in the countryside. There are cows in the fields. There's a rabbit scampering into the bushes. There are farms, which sell things on the roadside. We read the signs.

One says Potatoes for Sale, another says Daffodils, Two Dollars a Bunch, and the next one just says Puppies.

Puppies! Hey, wait a minute. Stop the car. Puppies! I want to see them. Dad stops the car. He looks at Mum.

Mum says, 'As long as you're happy just to look. We can't get a puppy now.'

I've already jumped out of the car. 'Come on,' I say.

An adventure wouldn't be an adventure if you didn't stop along the way to look at puppies. Mum takes a long time to get out of the car because of her roly poly belly.

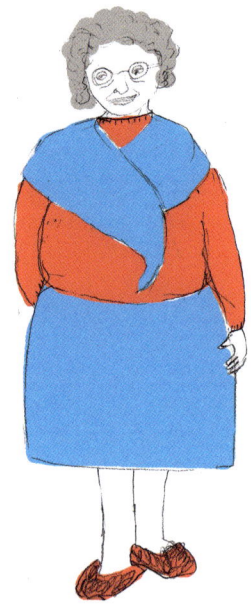

We knock on the door and a woman opens it. She's a bit roly poly herself. She takes us to her laundry and opens the door. There's a `whole basket full of puppies`, white and brown, and I want to cuddle them immediately.

When I kneel down, the puppies climb all over me. I'm like a waterfall of puppies. I'm covered with wet noses and soft ears and sharp little teeth. But there's a brown one in the corner that doesn't come close. It just looks at me.

'Come here…' I whisper, and I pat my knee very charmingly. It comes closer. I pat my knee again. Suddenly it bounds forward. I pick it up and give it a big snuggle. It nibbles my ear.

'Oh, if only I could take one home, this is the one I'd take.' I say this with a long, sad sigh. A sigh full of drama.

But Mum has had to sit down. And she's talking to Dad. And no one is paying me any attention at all. No one has even heard my long, sad sigh. The roly poly woman says, 'I reckon you're going to have a baby to take home, very soon.'

Then Dad says, 'Henrietta, I'm afraid we won't make it to the cousins. We have to take Mum home to have our baby. The baby is ready to come.'

'Now?'

Can it be true? Right in the middle of my adventure. This baby sister is very annoying. She's going to ruin my whole weekend. Now I'll never learn to ride a horse. Dad can see I'm disappointed.

'It will be exciting. You'll see. And we can go to the cousins another time soon, with our new baby.'

Somehow, I get the feeling this new baby is going to take up everyone's attention. Somehow, I'm not sure I want a baby sister after all. Even worse, now I have to say goodbye to my favourite brown puppy.

We get back in the car. Mum is having pains. Dad is driving fast. I'm eating popcorn and feeling miserable.

When we get home, Dad runs the bath and calls the midwife. At least I'm allowed to watch a movie for once, because everyone else is preparing for the baby to come. But the baby takes all day, and Dad and I eat the lasagne all by ourselves. Mum is too busy having a baby, so she can't eat. Dad is also pretty busy helping her have a baby. And even I start to feel a little bit excited at the thought of meeting my new baby sister.

Finally the baby arrives. Dad calls me in and tells me to come close. Mum is holding the baby. It looks all red and squished-up.

'Is that my baby sister?' I say.

'No, sweetheart, this is your baby brother,' says Mum. 'This is Albert.'

Oh boy! A baby brother. No wonder he's all red and squishy. I didn't want a baby brother. And already he has ruined my weekend. I sure hope he won't make a habit of it. I'm about to complain. I open my mouth, but then I see how happy my mum is, and how happy my dad is.

All their happiness comes straight at me, so I close my mouth and smile.

You just can't be sad when everyone else is happy, even if you didn't get to ride a horse or keep a puppy. Even though it's Albert who has arrived and not Alberta.

Mum tells me to sit down and she puts Albert in my arms.

'Hello, Albert,' I say and I give him a kiss. 'Welcome to the whirly old world.'

Albert doesn't even blink. He just says, 'Waaaaaaaaaa.'

Dad and I leave Mum and Albert to have a big sleep together, and we go outside just before dark. The apple tree has its new buds. Dad was right when he said the baby would come when the tree got its buds. It's a nice warm night for a baby to come. Dad asks me if

I'm pleased to have a baby brother. I have a think about this.

'It's strange that there's someone else to think about now in our family,' I say.

'Soon you'll have someone else to play with, too,' says Dad.

'When will he be old enough to play with?'

'After two Christmases.'

'That's even longer than waiting for him to be born!'

'True,' says Dad. 'But it went quickly, didn't it?'

I don't answer him. I can't even remember if it went quickly. The stars are beginning to shine in the sky. I feel as if life has just changed, as if one moment ago it was like it always was and now it's forever-after different. Now there's an Albert in our house. It's a funny feeling. A feeling as special and mysterious as stars.

Dad says, 'But because two years is a long time to wait, I thought maybe you and I should take a drive next weekend…'

'Where will we go?'

'We'll go get that brown puppy. Make sure you've got someone to play with till Albert is old enough.'

I jump up and down. I'm over the moon. What a night. What a perfect night. Now I'll have someone to look after, just like Mum and Dad. They can look after Albert, and I'll look after my brown puppy.

About the Author

Martine Murray was born in Melbourne and now lives in Castlemaine, Victoria. She has studied art and dabbled in acrobatics and dance, is an award-winning children's novelist and illustrator as well as a writer for adults, and has been published extensively overseas. *Henrietta: There's No One Better* was shortlisted for the NSW Premier's Literary Awards, Speech Pathology Australia Book of the Year Awards and APA Book Design Awards. *Henrietta and the Perfect Night* was a CBCA Honour Book.